William—The Rebel

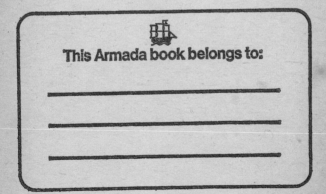

This Armada book belongs to:

Other titles by Richmal Crompton in Armada include:

William's Happy Days
William's Crowded Hours
William—The Detective
William—The Bad
Sweet William
Still—William
Just—William
William—The Bold
William—The Gangster
William Carries On
William—The Outlaw
William Again
More William
William In Trouble
William Does His Bit
William—The Pirate

First published in the U.K. in 1933
by George Newnes Ltd. and in this abridged edition in 1966

First published in Armada in 1977 by
Fontana Paperbacks, 14 St. James's Place, London, SW1A 1PF

Printed in Great Britain by
Love & Malcomson Ltd., Brighton Road,
Redhill, Surrey.

William—The Rebel

Richmal Crompton

Illustrated by Thomas Henry

Armada

CONTENTS

CHAPTER 1

THREE DOGS AND WILLIAM

THE whole trouble, of course, began with Ethel. Ethel had never had a dog, and there didn't seem to be any reason why Ethel should have a dog. She didn't like dogs. She didn't understand dogs. She had never felt that all-consuming urge to own a dog that assists in replenishing the coffers of the State. She disliked William's dog, Jumble, intensely, and regularly accused it of the destruction of any of her personal articles that she happened to have lost or mislaid. She was afraid of big dogs, and she said that little dogs made her feel sick . . .

When William heard, therefore, that Ethel was going to keep a dog he felt both surprised and indignant. Further investigation proved this decision to be the result of one of Ethel's bewildering swift affairs. A youth in the neighbourhood, who had conceived an ardent attachment for her, had, as a mark of that attachment, asked her to take charge of his Alsatian while he went on a holiday abroad. He had originally arranged for his sister to do this, but, having met Ethel and fallen beneath the spell of her blue eyes and red-gold hair, he had hastily cancelled the arrangement and given his pet into Ethel's charge, hoping thereby to bind her affection to him more deeply. Ethel was touched and gratified. She had lately been to see a film in which the heroine had possessed an Alsatian and had posed with it very effectively in a baronial hall and on the terrace steps of a large and park-like garden. Ethel's home had no baronial hall, its garden was devoid of terrace or steps, but she meant to reproduce the poses as best she could, and even improve on them. The young man, who evidently took the Alsatian (its name was Wotan) very seriously, gave her a long list of duties in connection with it. It had to be brushed and combed and cleaned and dosed and fed and exercised with alarming frequency. Moreover, it had to be exhibited at the local dog show, which was to take place in a week's time.

"He's a dead cert for a first prize," said the young man earnestly. "He'll want to be got ready properly, of course. I've just written down the few things I generally do to him before a show."

And he handed Ethel another long list of preparations. She felt depressed for a moment, but the young man had a straight nose and a nice smile, and she longed to try some of the poses that the girl on the pictures had used so effectively. Having seen that film, she would always now feel incomplete as a pretty girl without an Alsatian.

"Oh, I shall *love* to have him," she said brightly. "I *adore* dogs, you know."

It wasn't till the Alsatian had taken up his quarters in the house and the young man had actually set off for his holiday that Ethel realised the complications that would ensue from the meeting of Wotan and

Jumble as dwellers on the same hearth-stone. She had always looked upon Jumble as beneath contempt. She had imagined that Jumble would realise his inferiority in comparison with the noble Wotan and behave accordingly. But Jumble didn't seem to realise anything of the sort. Instead of welcoming the new guest with grateful obsequiousness, he greeted him with open hostility, snarling and growling and gathering himself together for an attack.

He was immediately ejected from the room, and William was ordered to keep him, in future, out of the new-comer's way.

"I like that," William muttered indignantly. "Yes, I *do* like that. Who came here first, I'd like to know —Jumble or that Wotan thing? Rotten he ought to be called. Well, I don't think it's fair. Jumble's got a *right* to his own home, hasn't he? S'pose someone came an' turned *you* out of your home an' said someone else must come in. How'd *you* like it?"

But Mrs. Brown supported Ethel. Mrs. Brown, too, was impressed by the aristocratic appearance of the Alsatian. Moreover, she always upheld the law of primogeniture.

"Ethel's the elder, William," she said, "so if the dogs can't live peaceably together then yours must go out of the house. Jumble's got his kennel and, anyway, he's never in the house much."

"He's in when I'm in," said William fiercely, "and it's his *home* an' he's had it all these years an' then you go an' turn him out for a rotten old thing that looks more like a donkey than a dog, anyway."

9

His mother, however, remained adamant, and Ethel was deaf to all his insults. She was enjoying the novelty of possessing a dog, and was combing and brushing and cleaning the creature with commendable assiduity. Moreover, she was practising the poses. It was, she found, more difficult to enter a room with one hand laid negligently on Wotan's head than anyone would have supposed. He had a way of suddenly withdrawing or hurrying forward at the psychological moment in a manner that completely spoilt the picture.

Still, she persevered, and certainly Wotan looked majestic and picturesque pacing by her side. William showed his displeasure by absenting himself completely from the house except for meals and sleep.

"If it's too good for Jumble," he said coldly, "it's too good for me. I don't want to stay in a place that's too good for Jumble. An' let me tell *you*, Jumble jolly well doesn't *want* to come into the house, so there! Not while that ole Rotten's here, anyway."

Jumble's behaviour, however, belied this statement. Jumble most decidedly did want to come into the house. Jumble knew that the house contained a rival and a foe, and he barked and growled defiance at it all day long, tugging at his lead when William led him past the door, straining at the kennel chain and snarling savagely when Ethel strolled past, her hand laid negligently on her new friend's head after the manner of the film heroine. Wotan ignored his presence, merely throwing a glance of haughty contempt in his direction as he passed. He seemed to look on Jumble as a creature with whom he could have no possible dealings. But there came a time of disillusionment and reckoning. For one afternoon Ethel sallied forth with her attendant hound without seeing first that Jumble was fastened up, and Jumble hurled himself upon the majestic Alsatian with the pent-up fury of many days. The Alsatian had evidently conceived a deeper dislike of Jumble than he had allowed to appear in his demeanour. He returned the attack with interest, snapping with such vigour that, when the dogs were finally separated by William and the gardener, Jumble had to be taken to the vet to have his side stitched up. The vet decided to keep Jumble for a few days. He had had much past experience of William's amateur surgery.

William returned home dogless and disconsolate. Ethel, of course, said that it was entirely Jumble's fault.

"Wotan didn't do a *thing* to Jumble till Jumble flew at him."

"Oh, didn't he!" said William bitterly. "Well, let me tell you it was *all* that ole Rotten's fault. How would *you* like to be turned out of your house and have someone else carrying on as if it belonged to them? I suppose *you'd* jus' sit quiet in a kennel an' do nothin'! Huh!"

He tried to annoy the majestic Wotan by pulling faces at him or making provocative noises, but Wotan ignored him completely. Wotan was now the pampered darling of the household. Ethel scented his hair and tied blue ribbon round his neck. Mr. Brown bought him an indiarubber bone as a plaything, but Wotan sniffed at it disdainfully, then turned away.

11

Wotan was not the type of dog that plays with india-rubber bones . . .

*   *   *   *   *

William walked slowly and desolately along the road. Each Jumble-less day seemed like a month to him. Jumble led an adventurous life, and it was not the first time that he had had to retire for a few days into the vet's charge. It was not that that gave the situation its peculiar bitterness. It was the sight of Jumble's rival and assailant in possession of the house and garden that William looked upon as belonging by right to his own pet.

He slouched along, his hands in his pockets, his toes dragging in the dust.

"That ole Rotten!" he muttered disconsolately. "Huh! Hung for murder, that's what he ought to be, 'stead of havin' indiarubber bones an' such-like given him!"

He turned round to gaze with deep self-pity at the empty space at his heels where Jumble normally trotted along behind him, then stood still in amazement. A small white dog was trotting along behind him. It wasn't Jumble. It was smaller, rougher, even more suggestive of a mongrel than Jumble, but it trotted at William's heels as if it belonged to him; it stopped when he stopped, and wagged its tail, gazing trustfully up at his face.

"Good old chap!" said William, and the little white dog curvetted ecstatically about his feet. William began to walk on again and, glancing carelessly over his shoulder, was much gratified to find that the little white dog still followed. He pretended to himself that Wotan did not exist, and that he and Jumble were walking home together after a morning's rabbiting in the wood. This mental picture, however, was rudely shattered by reality, for at a bend of the road there appeared Ethel, walking slowly along with Wotan, one hand resting on his head in painstaking imitation of the pose. She looked disappointed to find that the turn of the road revealed no other spectator than William. As William approached he fixed a deliberately contemptuous gaze upon the lordly Wotan.

"Huh!" he muttered scornfully as he came abreast with them.

Suddenly all was pandemonium. The small white dog, evidently mistaking William's contemptuous "Huh!" for a new form of "Sick him!" gave a low growl and sprang forthwith upon the astonished Wotan. The battle was short and inglorious, and in less than a minute Wotan was fleeing down the road, pursued by a small white tornado. A torn and trampled blue ribbon was left to mark the battle-field. Ethel, who had screamed hysterically while the fray was going on, now snatched up the trampled blue ribbon and ran off, still screaming, after her pet. William stood and watched with a smile of quiet enjoyment . . .

Soon the little white dog reappeared, running back along the road. He was obviously very much pleased both with himself and William. He leapt joyfully up at William, then took his place again at his heels, trotting demurely along.

Life had now taken on a new aspect for William.

13

All his dejection had left him. He had a dog, a super dog, a dog who could turn the noble and majestic Wotan into a fleeing streak of lightning. Life was worth living again, gloriously, hilariously worth living.

He swaggered up to the front gate, his new friend still trotting trustingly at his heels. Mrs. Brown was there waiting for him.

"William," she said, "it's very unkind of you to set strange dogs on to Wotan like this. It's upset Ethel very much."

"I didn't set a strange dog on it," said William. "I didn't set any dog on it. My dog was jus' trying to have a game with it, but that ole Rotten's such a coward."

"Your dog?" said Mrs. Brown. "But Jumble's at the vet's . . ."

Then suddenly she saw the little white dog looking up at her, wagging its tail ingratiatingly.

"William!" she said dismayed. "*Whatever's* this?"

"That?" said William carelessly. "That's my new dog."

"You *can't* have another dog, William," said Mrs. Brown firmly, "you've got one."

"Well, it's at the vet's, an' I want a dog to be going on with. I want two, anyway. If Ethel can have one as big as that ole Rotten I ought to have about six ordinary size ones to make up."

"Well, you can't, William," said Mrs. Brown. "I'm absolutely *sick* of dogs," she added fervently, "and I'm dreading the time when Jumble comes back to make more trouble. You mustn't *dream* of keeping this dog."

"I'm not keeping it," said William, astutely changing his point of attack. "I can't stop it following me, can I? I've done all I can to stop it following me an' it isn't any good, so I'll jus' have to put up with it."

"You can't keep it, William," said his mother firmly. "I'll go and ring up the police now, and see if a dog's been lost."

Rather to her disappointment, it turned out that no dog had been lost. Mrs. Brown asked the police to come and fetch the dog, but the police politely refused to do this. She had apparently given the dog shelter, and therefore she was responsible. If she sent the animal in question to the police station they would receive it, but they would not come and fetch it.

"You can take it to the police station or get rid of it some other way, William," said Mrs. Brown; "but I simply won't have it here."

Thoughtfully William walked away, followed happily, trustingly, by his new friend. Half an hour later he returned alone, wearing his famous expression of imbecile virtue.

"I've got rid of it," he said.

"Did you take it to the police station?" asked his mother.

"No. I got rid of it on the way," said William. "I thought that was the best thing to do. I jus' got it lost on the way."

"I am very glad you did, dear," said Mrs. Brown, much relieved, and gave him a large piece of cake, which he took to the old barn and shared with the little white dog who was tied up in the farthest corner of it.

The little white dog seemed to take quite happily to his new existence. During the day he roamed the fields and woods with William, staying in the old barn when William had to go home for meals, and spending the night in the tumble-down summer-house that no one ever used at the bottom of the Browns' garden. He seemed to thrive on the odd mixture of scraps, purloined from the Browns' larder, that now formed his staple diet. One would have thought that he had never known any other existence than this, any other master than William. William discovered that, though docile and friendly ordinarily, he turned into a little tempest of ferocity when "sicked" on to fight. He had the courage of a dog twice his size—and a brave dog at that. William longed to bring about a decisive combat between Wotan and his new pet, but to advertise his new pet's existence in this way would be to secure his final dismissal.

The day of the show was drawing near, and Ethel was intent upon the preparations for it. Wotan was brushed, combed, cleaned, dosed and dieted with renewed energy. He was given a tonic to steady his nerves for the ordeal. He slept on a specially prepared bed, raised from the ground in order not to expose his precious person to draughts. A new length of blue ribbon was brought for him. William suspected that Ethel's heart was not in these preparations, although she carried them out so conscientiously. The novelty of possessing an Alsatian was wearing off. She had been again to the pictures and seen a film whose heroine played with a kitten in a way that made the only two possible poses with Wotan seem

16

extremely dull. Moreover, the memory of Wotan's owner was growing dim, and she had now met another young man—with an even straighter nose and nicer smile than Wotan's owner's—who wasn't interested in dogs. Still—she was intensely anxious for the kudos of Wotan's victory. She felt that she would be dis-

Through the hedge the two of them were watching with interest the final preparation of Wotan.

17

honoured for ever if Wotan failed to win his first prize.

The day of the show arrived. Wotan, brushed, combed, sleek and shining, his neck adorned by an enormous length of brand-new ribbon, was led out by Ethel into the back garden. Ethel wore a new hat and looked rather nervous.

"Jus' stay there a minute, sweetie 'ickle man," she said, "while mummie goes to fetch a keen hanky."

Despite her affectionate tone of voice she looked at him rather coldly. There was something very unresponsive about Wotan. She had never really been able to establish contact with him. A kitten would be much more satisfactory in every way.

She had no idea, of course, that that little scene had an audience. William happened to be passing the house with his white dog and, as always, was skirting it furtively by way of the field that bordered the back garden, so as not to expose his pet to the eyes of his unsuspecting family. Through the hedge the two of them were watching with interest the final preparation of Wotan. Ethel gave the blue ribbon a final tweak.

"Doesn't he look a pretty ickle boykins!" she said, laying her cheek against his head.

Wotan continued to gaze blankly into space.

Ethel sighed wistfully and went indoors. Wotan continued to gaze into space. The sight of him sitting there in sole possession of the garden from which he had ousted both Jumble and the little white dog, the smugness and conceit and stupidity of the expression with which he gazed around it, was more than William could endure.

Before he realised what he was doing he had whispered a quiet, low "S'k". The small white tornado shot through the hedge and flung itself upon the nonchalant giant. The giant, dropping his nonchalance, put up a fairly good fight, but he was no match for the white tornado. He fled yelping round and round the garden, pursued by his valiant little foe. Once more his blue ribbon was torn and trampled. One ear hung bleeding. There was a deep scratch down one flank. In his wild efforts to escape he knocked over a watering-can of water and rolled over on the rose-bed. Gone was his perfumed elegance . . . He was muddy, dirty, and bleeding—no object for a dog show or indeed for a public appearance of any sort. Ethel, drawn by the growls and snarls, came running into the garden. William called off his pet, but not before Ethel had seen it. They hastily departed, leaving Ethel moaning over her fallen hero.

William did not come home that night till bedtime. Ethel had gone to bed in a state of nervous collapse. Wotan sat on the dining-room hearth-rug, wearing his bandages with an air of mournful pride. William was at once taxed, as he knew he would be, on the subject of the little white dog. He had prepared an attitude of complete innocence that sounded less convincing than he had hoped it would sound.

"That dog? Which dog? Oh, yes, I remember. That dog that followed me some days ago. Well, I told you, didn't I? I lost it. I lost it when I was takin' it to the police station. Yes . . . now you mention it, I *do* think I've seen it about once or twice since. Yes, I have seen it about . . . but I can't help that, can I? I can't stop dogs walkin' about in the world if they want to, can I? Was it that dog that went for ole Rotten? I'm not sure whether it was or not . . . yes, I happened to be jus' in the field an'—yes, now you mention it, I did see a dog go for ole Rotten, but how can *I* tell whether it was that dog what followed me an' what I lost? I don't know every dog in the world, do I? I don't see how I can, consid'rin' there mus' be thousands an' thousands of them.

"Anyway, it isn't anythin' to do with me, is it, if that ole Rotten can't stick up for himself? . . . I tell you I don't know what white dog it was. I only jus' happened to see a white dog goin' for him. I keep tellin' you I don't know all the white dogs in the world . . ."

But he was aware that he did not deceive them. As he went to bed he decided that until their suspicions were lulled he must find other night's lodging for the little white dog than the summer-house. He woke very early next morning and at once went to look out of the window. To his horror and amazement he saw a man in leggings, carrying a gun, walking towards the summer-house. He recognised him as the gamekeeper from the Hall. He realised at once what had happened. His father had discovered the dog in the summer-house last night and, urged on by Ethel, had asked the gamekeeper to come round and shoot it first thing in the morning. Without stopping even to put on his slippers, William hurled himself downstairs and into the garden. He next proceeded to hurl himself upon the gamekeeper. The gamekeeper, however, was not attempting to shoot anything, for the simple reason that there was nothing to be shot. The summer-house was empty. William stared at it in surprise. Only last night he had safely secured his pet in it. He must have got out through the window that William always left open for ventilation. At that moment there came sudden signs of consternation from the house. The housemaid had come down to find the silver gone and signs everywhere of the recent presence of a burglar. A scream from Ethel proclaimed that her jewellery had gone. Meantime, the lordly Wotan slept peacefully upon his patent raised bed. The gamekeeper searched the bushes and outhouse, prepared to shoot small white dogs and burglars indiscriminately. Mr. Brown, clad in his pyjamas and armed with a poker, rang up the police . . . Gradually quiet ensued, and the family went to dress.

In the middle of breakfast there came a telephone call from the police. The burglar had been found with the spoils upon him. He had evidently been tracked and was being held at bay by a small white dog. The small white dog was keeping him in one spot, snapping at him ferociously whenever he attempted to move, and barking loudly to attract attention. Two policemen brought the spoils back to the Browns' house. At their heels trotted proudly the small white dog.

"Well," said William, "surely now he's saved all your lives and the silver *and* Ethel's pearls—surely you'll let me keep him *now*."

But Mr. Brown was reading out an advertisement from the morning paper. "Lost, probably in neighbourhood of Marleigh, small white dog, answering to the name of Tinker. Reward offered."

As one man the Brown family rose and went to the open window, outside which sat the little dog, gazing up expectantly.

"Tinker!' said the Brown family simultaneously. There was no doubt as to the little white dog's response. He hurled himself up at the window with every sign of ecstasy.

Mr. Brown at once got into communication with the telephone number given in the advertisement and was informed that the advertiser would come at once, arriving early in the afternoon.

The various members of the family spent the intervening hours in various ways.

Ethel spent it taking Wotan to his owner's sister.

"I'm afraid I can't look after him any longer," she said sweetly. "I simply *adore* him, but I'm just simply too busy to look after him any longer. Yes, I'm so sorry about the show yesterday. He had a fight and couldn't be shown. Yes, it was very unfortunate."

She left Wotan sitting on the drawing-room hearthrug, still staring majestically in front of him, and went down to Marleigh to enquire the price of kittens . . . playful kittens . . . the sort the girl on the pictures had had . . .

William spent the morning in sorrowful company with the little white dog. Its charms seemed to multiply as the hour of its departure drew near. William didn't know how he was going to part with it . . .

Mrs. Brown spent the morning removing the traces of the burglar's feet from the hall linoleum and his fingermarks from the furniture.

Early in the afternoon a young man arrived. He and the little white dog greeted each other with rapture.

"I'd sooner have lost anything in the world than this fellow," said the young man, holding the little white dog affectionately in his arms. "I brought him back with me from Africa. He's the world's best hunting dog. He can hold up a lion or a leopard anywhere—keep out of his way, but simply hold him to the same spot, just as if he'd got him tied up. He's a pretty valuable little chap, too. There aren't many of his breed about. I was motoring with him past here on my way to London last week, and I suppose he must have fallen or jumped out from the back of the car. I'm joly glad to see him again, I can tell you. Let me see . . . who actually found him?"

William, of course, had actually found him, so the young man gave William a five-pound note. This was little compensation to William for the loss of the little white dog. In any case five pounds was too large a sum to be of any use to William. It would, he knew, be confiscated by his father and put to swell his post office savings account—a procedure that William regarded as a shameless, deliberate swindle.

Ethel's blue eyes and red-gold hair were having their wonted effect upon the young man.

"I'm awfully grateful to you for being so good to my little chap," he said fervently.

"Oh, I *adored* him," said Ethel, fluttering her tawny

23

lashes entrancingly; "we *all* adored him. We shall miss him horribly."

"I can see you're a dog lover all right," said the young man, his admiration deepening.

"I adore dogs," said Ethel unblushingly, as she mentally relinquished the playful kitten in favour of a small white dog.

"Of course, most people think he's a mongrel," said the young man.

"Oh, I knew at *once* that he wasn't a mongrel," Ethel assured him.

William exchanged a slow wink with the little white dog.

The young man had driven off at last with his dog, after arranging to call and take Ethel out for a drive one day next week.

William was left alone to consider the situation. The house was clear of Wotan—that was one good thing. But it was also clear of his little white friend, which was not so good. Still . . . William could not help seeing that there were redeeming factors in the situation. He would insist on having at least five shillings of his five pounds in hand. And—he felt relieved that Jumble's courage was no longer under a cloud, as he had secretly felt it to be ever since he had been so ingloriously chewed up by Wotan. After all—you couldn't expect Jumble to be just like a dog trained to "bay" lions and leopards. No, Jumble was certainly as brave as any ordinary dog possibly could be. His affection rushed out towards his faithful pet, who had gone through so many adventures with him. He wondered how he could possibly have lived all this week without him. He wondered how he could possibly have thought that even the little white dog could take his place. He suddenly remembered that the vet had said Jumble might be able to come home to-day.

Whistling loudly and untunefully, he set off down the road at a run towards the vet's home.

CHAPTER II

A RESCUE PARTY

"WHAT I think's so awful," said William, seated firmly on one of his favourite hobby-horses, "is that I've lived all these years and not *done* anything yet."

"You've done quite enough," said his mother. "You've broken every window in the house at one time or another, you've made the geyser explode twice, you've *ruined* the parquet by sliding on it, and you've got tar all over the hall carpet."

"Well, I can't help them putting tar on the roads, can I?" said William, stung by the injustice of this accusation. "I've got to walk somewhere, haven't I? I can't fly, can I? It's not fair to blame *me* because people put tar on the roads. Besides, I didn't mean that sort of thing, anyway. I meant the sort of thing that makes you famous. The sort of thing people put up statues to you for. I meant, it's awful to think of me living all these years an' not done anythin' yet to make the world ring with my name."

"The world'll ring with your name all right," said William's elder brother, who had entered the room in the middle of William's diatribe. "I bet you any money we'll all live to see you hung."

William ignored this remark except for a withering glance of which he was secretly rather proud.

"What I mean is," he continued to his mother, "that with wastin' all my time in school like what I have to, I never have any left to do anythin' to make the world ring with my name. I bet I'd've been famous by now if I hadn't had to waste all my time in school."

"One might almost say you're famous now," put in Robert, who had remained unwithered by William's withering glance. "At least, everyone for miles around knows there's some sort of trouble coming as soon as he sees you. I suppose that's fame in a way."

"What could you have done, dear?" said Mrs. Brown hastily to William, seeing him preparing to meet this challenge.

"I'd have invented something," he said, his attention drawn once more to his wrongs. "Look at all the things that've been invented by other people while I've been wastin' my time in school. I did invent somethin' to stop Mrs. Bott's chimney smokin', but there must've been somethin' wrong with the chimney. The *invention* was all right. Or I'd have caught crim'nals. I bet I'd be jolly good catching crim'nals, only I never get a chance to try. I bet I'd've had a statue put up to me for catchin' crim'nals by now if I'd not had to waste all my time in school."

At this moment Mrs. Bott was announced, and Robert made a hasty exit. William stayed behind, not because he derived any pleasure from Mrs. Bott's society, but because he wished to continue his conversation with his mother as soon as the visitor should have departed. He had thought of a lot of exploits by which he might have made his name famous if he

27

had not been forced to waste the precious hours of his youth in school. He might have discovered a new continent. He might have tamed a jungle full of lions. He might even have got into communication with Mars . . .

"I bet there'd have been hundreds of statues up to me all over the world by now," he muttered indignantly.

"What do you say, dear?" said Mrs. Bott, who was slightly deaf.

"Nothin'," said William morosely.

His mother glanced at him apprehensively.

"Don't you want to go out and play, William?" she said.

"No, thanks," said William.

"Hadn't you better be getting on with your homework, then?" said Mrs. Brown, who had no wish to resume the unending discussion on the uselessness of school. It was a perennial source of contention and each knew the other's arguments by heart.

"Homework!" echoed William and uttered a hollow laugh.

Mrs. Bott looked at him with interest.

"I think he needs a dose, dear," she said to Mrs. Brown. "I believe in Gregory powder myself. It's old-fashioned, I know, but there's nothing like it for these bilious attacks."

William threw her a glance before which—in his imaginary exploits—strong men had quailed. Mrs. Bott met it unflinchingly.

"Bilious," she said with deepening interest to Mrs. Brown; "you can see it in every line of his face."

Without a word William walked slowly and majestically out of the room. But he lingered in the hall within earshot in case they should begin to discuss him. They didn't, however, somewhat to his disappointment. Instead Mrs. Bott said:

"I was going to ask you to come to tea with me next week, dear. Botty's gone up to Scotland for a little holiday, and I'm that lonely . . ."

William walked abruptly away. He wasn't interested in Mr. Bott (always alluded to by his wife as Botty), the short, stout manufacturer of Bott's Sauce, who lived at the Hall, and whose generosity compensated in the eyes of the neighbourhood for his lack of education and his frequent omission of the letter H.

He wasn't interested in Mr. Bott, and he wasn't interested in Mrs. Bott—large, florid, golden-haired, vulgar and good-natured. He was only interested in himself and his frustrated frame.

"Eleven years old," he muttered bitterly to the umbrella stand, "and not done a *thing* with my life but sums an' g'ography an' stuff like that."

Then quite suddenly he made up his mind. He'd run away and seek his fortune. Not a minute more of his life must be wasted. He'd set out now this minute. Before him lay the world, holding at every turn innumerable promises of fame and fortune. He'd walk to the sea, keeping an eye open for adventures on the way, of course, and there he'd join a band of pirates. He'd make himself master of the pirates and discover a new continent, then, having conquered the natives, he'd make himself king. After that he'd train his conquered natives till they were the finest army in

*William crammed as many into his
pockets as they would hold.*

the world and then there wasn't any reason why he shouldn't conquer the whole world. All this would take time, of course, and he hadn't a moment to lose.

The first immediate necessity was provisions for his journey. Cautiously he entered the larder and, finding a pile of meat pasties on a plate there, crammed as many into his pockets as they would hold. These simple preparations completed, he put on his cap and set off jauntily down the road. Rather to his disappointment he reached Marleigh, three miles distant, without adventure. Outside Marleigh he sat down and, though it was only a short time since he had had his tea, ate the meat pasties. He meant to eat one only, but somehow he had finished them before he realised it. One had broken into tiny pieces in his pocket, but William was no whit disconcerted by this. He ate every fragment, including a piece of string, some bits of crayon, a small piece of rubber, and a generous sprinkling of ant's eggs, a packet of which, destined for his goldfish, had lately broken in his pocket. Cheered and refreshed by this mixed diet, he set off once more. He did not know the country beyond Marleigh, and he went slowly and warily, as a man might go in a lion-infested jungle. He would be disappointed to meet with no adventure before he reached the sea. A cow stared at him mournfully over a hedge, and he returned its gaze suspiciously, as if it might turn out after all to be some wild animal in disguise. But it remained indubitably a cow, and William walked on, depressed and disappointed by the ordinariness of life. Suddenly he brightened . . . A high wall ran along the roadside, and behind the wall, some distance from the road, William could see the chimneys of a large house. He looked up to the top of the wall. A row of broken glass bottles embedded in cement crowned it . . . The sinister aspect of this struck William at once. Here was his adventure ready to hand. He must find out what nefarious design was being hatched behind this grim fortification and bring the perpetrators to justice. That surely would give him fame . . . It would probably indeed lead to the offer of a high appointment at Scotland Yard. William decided to accept the appointment when it was offered to him . . .

He wandered round the wall till he came to a small wooden gate. He tried it, and to his delight it yielded. He entered a picturesque kitchen garden. Seeing two gardeners at work on a vegetable bed in the distance, he crept cautiously along by the inside of the wall till he came to a yew hedge that separated the kitchen garden from the garden proper. He squeezed through this with a certain amount of difficulty, deciding *en route* that the taste of a yew hedge was inferior to the taste of hawthorn, privet, or beech (William was a connoisseur in the taste of hedges), and found himself on a spacious lawn. The house was now revealed to him—large, square, ivy-covered. Its largeness and squareness gave it a satisfactorily sinister and prison-like appearance. There was a line of shrubs at the side of the lawn, and under cover of this William made his cautious way to the house, then began very warily to peep into the windows. The first room he inspected was a handsomely appointed drawing-room, the second a handsomely appointed dining-room, the next a kitchen . . . William hurried past this. He had learnt by experience that the inhabitants of the kitchen are apt to be particularly unceremonious in the treatment of small boys found loitering on the premises. The next room was a small study, in which a man sat writing at a table. William thought that he had the look of a man who was head of a gang . . . He walked on to the window of the next room, then stood, paralysed with amazement, eyes and mouth wide open. For there on a table, clad only in his vest and pants, lay Mr. Bott—Mr. Bott, who was supposed to be in Scotland! And that was not all. For a tall, grim-looking man in a white coat was engaged in savagely pulling Mr. Bott's arms and legs, first an arm and then a leg, in a way that was obviously designed to force them out of their sockets. At each jerk Mr. Bott screwed up his face in agony.

"Torcher!" said William to himself, with mingled horror and satisfaction. "They've captured him on his way to Scotland, and now they're torcherin' him . . ."

He would have liked to watch longer, but a sense of personal danger made him reluctantly tear himself away.

He returned to the road, and there stood still for a moment to consider the situation. There was no need now to run away to sea. Here was fame ready to hand. By freeing Mr. Bott from the nest of kidnappers and torcherers, by exposing and bringing to justice the whole gang of them, surely he would become so celebrated that Scotland Yard would ask him to lend them his services. He decided that he would only lend them on condition that he was made one of the Big Five.

He was aware, of course, that the situation must be carefully handled. To begin with, he wasn't going to let the police in on it. They would take all the credit to themselves. On further consideration he decided not to let any grown-up in on it. Grown-ups were notoriously ungrateful. If there were any credit to be got out of the *coup*, they would get it themselves and pretend that he'd not done anything. He uttered a scornful laugh. Huh! He knew grown-ups by this time . . . They'd do all they could to keep him out of the Big Five. He walked homewards thoughtfully. The difficulties of the situation seemed to increase as he pondered on them. He had, of course, more than once discovered what he thought were gangs of criminals, but subsequent events had proved that his imagination played a rather too large part in the affair. Always the "criminals" he had discovered had turned out to be ordinary law-abiding citizens. But this was different. He had with his own ears heard Mrs. Bott declare that her husband had gone to Scotland. He had with his own eyes seen Mr. Bott not five miles from his own home, being manhandled by his captor in a large, prison-like house . . . There could be no possible mistake this time. But he must go carefully. Though he had no small opinion of his own physical and mental powers, he realised that he must have assistance of some sort to manage the affair successfully. He decided to consult his Outlaws. They might be able to help him evolve some plan.

He went slowly to the old barn which was his head-quarters, and where he was more likely to find his Outlaws than anywhere else. He found them, accompanied by a large crowd of their schoolmates, playing "French and English". Left to themselves, the Outlaws had very little imagination in the matter of games. At first William was disconcerted not to find them alone, then he brightened, realising the possibilities of the situation. He would take all these boys with him to rescue Mr. Bott. Though small, they would surely by sheer numbers overpower the jailer in the white coat and release the prisoner . . . Moreover, unlike grown-ups, they would not try to steal the credit from him. He was their accepted leader. They were accustomed to follow him. Already he felt himself a general leading his troops to victory.

Ginger greeted him somewhat shamefacedly, aware that "French and English" was not quite worthy of his powers of invention.

"Hello," he said; "you weren't here and there didn't seem anything else to play at . . ."

"I'm going to make a speech," said William, dragging out of the old barn the packing-case that usually formed his rostrum. Ginger, assuming his usual function of William's aide-de-camp, made a funnel with his two hands, and shouted: "William's going to make a speech."

The boys stopped playing and crowded round the packing-case, repeating the shout: "William's going to make a speech."

William mounted his precarious stand.

"Ladies and gentlemen," he began. There were no ladies present, but William always considered that the correct opening for a speech in all circumstances. "Ladies and gentlemen . . ."

This opening was conscientiously applauded by his followers, and, clearing his throat, he continued:

"You've all gotter come an' rescue someone—some-one what's in prison havin' his arms an' legs pulled out what his wife thought was in Scotland all the time. Well, how would you like your arms an' legs pulled out when your wife thought you were in Scot-land? What I mean to say is that when we find people pullin' other people's arms an' legs out we oughter *stop* it. It's an unkind thing to do, an' we oughtn't to do unkind things like the good Samaritan in the Bible. I bet if you go with me to where this man is—havin' his arms an' legs pulled out by a man in a white coat —we'll jolly well rescue him an' stop people in white coats pullin' other people's arms an' legs out, 'cause it's a very wrong thing to do. Pullin' arms an' legs out is forbidden by lor. I'm goin' to Scotland Yard when we've done this rescue an' I'll give any of you a job as policeman when you're old enough. You can't have quite such a high-up job as mine. Stands to reason you can't, 'cause it was me what found this man in the white coat pullin' his arms an' legs out, an' it's me what's goin' to take you to rescue this man what's arms an' legs are bein' pulled out."

He paused for breath, and thunderous applause broke out. They were not quite sure what it was all about. They were clear only on one point, and that was that William was going to lead them to adven-ture. They were heartily tired of "French and English", and welcomed any change. Gratified by the reception of his speech, William continued with rising elo-quence:

36

"What we've gotter think of is this: Would we like our own arms an' legs pulled out by a man in a white coat? An' if we wouldn't, then——"

Further speech was drowned by a large report as the packing-case gave way beneath him, precipitating him among the *débris*.

But there was no need for him to continue. Already the rescuers were eagerly preparing themselves for battle, seizing even upon the fragments of his erstwhile platform as weapons, and brandishing them above their heads. He crept out from the *débris*, removed a nail from his hair, a piece of wood from his mouth, and several splinters from his hands. He then examined his knees with interest.

"I bet I'm goin' to have a bruise as big as a football on this knee," he said. "Well, that *shows*, doesn't it?" he continued, turning the episode skilfully to account. "If jus' fallin' off a box hurts as much as this, what mus' it hurt like to have your arms an' legs pulled out? . . . Well, who's coming to this place where they capture people goin' to Scotland an' pull their arms an' legs out?"

They were all coming apparently. Already Ginger was marshalling the band. Already miniature battles were taking place with pieces of packing-case as weapons.

"Come on, then," said William, slipping one hand inside his jacket in faithful imitation of the picture of Napoleon that formed the frontispiece of his history book. "Come on. We don't want to find him with no arms or legs left when we get there . . ."

Eagerly the band set off. One boy produced a

whistle from his pocket and blew it lustily as he walked. Another ran into his house, which they passed on the way, and came out with a tin tray, which he beat jubilantly with a stick.

William, however, sternly forbade these exuberant manifestations of the martial spirit. "D'you want them to *know* we're coming?" he said indignantly. "D'you want to give them the alarm so's they'll clear off to the Cont'nent with him an' when we get there we'll jus' find an empty house? Haven't you got any *sense*?"

The crestfallen musicians meekly put aside their instruments and walked on in (comparative) silence.

Outside the wooden gate in the high brick wall William addressed them again in sibilant tones, his collar turned up with fine conspiratorial effect, and wearing the tense frown of one who engages upon a desperate undertaking.

"Now, listen," he said. "This man's imprisoned here by a gang what captured him when he was going to Scotland. They're torcherin' him in here, pullin' his arms an' legs out, an' what we've gotter do is rescue him. Give me that whistle."

The owner of the whistle meekly gave it to him.

"Now you come with me to a hedge here, an' I'll go an' scout to find out where he is, an' then when I whistle you mus' all run out and rescue him . . ."

Fortunately for the band of rescuers, the kitchen garden was empty. Following William, they crept through to the cover of the yew hedge and there William again addressed them in the sibilant whisper.

"Now you stay here an' wait," he said, "an' I'll

go'n' scout, an' remember when I whistle all run out an' rescue him."

He crept along the edge of the lawn till he reached a copper beech, beneath which a garden roller made a convenient step. In less than a minute he had swung himself up from the roller into the branches and had crept along the lowest one as far as he dared, in order to keep his look out upon the house and garden. At present there was nothing of interest to see in either. The garden was empty. The downstairs rooms were empty . . . Then suddenly Mr. Bott came out of the house and began to wander about the garden. He looked morose and miserable. He heaved deep sighs as he walked . . . William formed his plans quickly. He would wait till Mr. Bott reached the spot just beneath his branch. Then he would blow his whistle, drop down, and with his band of rescuers rush the prisoner to the door in the wall and thence homeward. Mr. Bott paced slowly on towards the tree. He came beneath William's branch. William blew his whistle and dropped. The drop was only partially successful. He had meant to land just in front of Mr. Bott. Instead he landed on the top of Mr. Bott. The two of them rolled on to the ground, Mr. Bott struggling violently and shouting: "Help, help! Murder! Fire! Thieves!" The band of rescuers leapt upon him, pulling him, pushing him, dragging him by his coat, hustling him from all sides.

"Help, help!" shouted Mr. Bott again. "I'm being murdered!"

"Shut up," ordered William fiercely. "Can't you

see you're being *rescued*? Shut up an' come on. We're *rescuin'* you, I tell you."

Mr. Bott, however, continued to struggle with his rescuers, and soon the man in the white coat was seen running across the lawn from the house. During the mêlée that followed William came to the conclusion that his opinion of the physical prowess of his contemporaries had been unduly optimistic. The noble band of rescuers was scattered by a few well-aimed blows from the new-comer's fists and a few well-aimed kicks from his boots. They fled in panic before him, pushing each other from behind in their eagerness to reach the wooden door.

"And if you come in here again with your monkey tricks," shouted the man, "I'll wring your necks— every one of you."

"Huh!" said William, picking himself up from the road where his hasty exit had landed him. "Yes, I bet he'd wring our necks all right . . . Well, doesn't that *prove* he's a torcherer like what I said? Who'll come back an' try again?"

But nobody wanted to do that. The rescuers had had their fill of rescuing—for the present, at any rate. They had enjoyed the adventure on the whole, but as an adventure, it was now perfect and complete. To add to it in any way would be to gild the lily. So they marched back, blowing the whistle and beating the tray to their hearts' content.

"I bet we'll have scared him," said Ginger. "I bet he'll let him go now. I bet we've jolly well rescued him."

The rescuers enthusiastically adopted this attitude

40

as one that satisfied honour and exempted them from again encountering the fists and boots of the man in the white coat.

"We've rescued him," they chanted to the accompaniment of the whistle and the tin tray; "we've jolly well rescued him."

William felt less sure on this point. But he realised that some other method must now be tried. He had underestimated the intelligence of Mr. Bott (who had not even the sense to recognise rescuers when he saw them) and the physical prowess of the white-coated torcherer. For a few minutes he was at a loss. Then his face cleared. The wronged wife, unaware that her husband was in the hands of kidnappers and torturers . . . She would surely feel enough gratitude to one who discovered the plot to see that he received his due reward. Mrs. Bott, though devoid of most of the graces conferred by breeding and education, was generous to a fault. She was, moreover, touchingly, childishly credulous. She would not pooh-hooh his story as most grown-ups would, and so waste valuable time and give the villains opportunity to escape. He dismissed his hilarious band (still blowing the whistle and beating the tray) and set out purposefully for the Hall.

A disapproving butler opened the door. Mrs Bott's butler had once butlered a duke and despised all Mrs. Bott's visitors on principle, but there was more than his normal disapproval in his eye when it fell upon William.

William, indeed, fresh from his exploit of attempted rescue, was not a reassuring sight. His hair stood on end, his collar was burst open, his tie hung under one ear. He was covered with garden soil where a blow from the man in the white coat had landed him neatly into the shrubbery. Laurel leaves adorned his hair.

In fact, Mrs. Bott's butler's indignation was such that he found it difficult to retain the official calm upon which he prided himself. To have sunk to Trade was bad enough, but to have such objects presenting themselves upon one's front door-step . . . He closed his eyes and a spasm of pain passed over his chiselled features.

"Do you know where the back door is?" he said in a hollow voice, opening his eyes, only to close them again with another spasm.

"Yes," said William in unsuspecting friendliness. " 'Course I do. Have you got lost? I'll show you if you like. But I want to see Mrs. Bott first."

"Mrs. Bott?" said the butler in a faint, suffering voice.

"Yes," said William, pushing his way unceremoniously into the hall.

"Have you an appointment?" said the butler, gathering his scattered forces.

"Lots," said William, putting on a careless swagger in order to hide his ignorance of the meaning of the word.

Wincing, the butler collected a few laurel leaves from William's hair and dropped them with ostentatious disdain on the front door-step.

"Don't you bother about me," said William, touched by this attention. "I don't mind a few leaves an' things about me. Is she in the drawing-room?"

"Mrs. Bott is not at liberty," said the butler.

"Yes, she is," said William; "it's *him* what isn't. That's what I've come about. Where is she?"

"I've already told you——" began the butler.

"Well, I can't stop here chattering with you like this," said William kindly. "I'm busy."

He pushed past the butler and made his way into the drawing-room.

Mrs. Bott was lying on the sofa, reading a novel. She looked up as William entered and gazed at his dishevelled figure in alarm.

"Whatever mischief have you been in now, William?" she said. "I never saw such a sight as you look. I am sorry for your poor mother. I am reely."

"He's bein' torchered," said William abruptly.

"What?" gasped Mrs. Bott.

"He's bein' torchered," repeated William. "He's having his arms an' legs pulled out."

"Now, William," said Mrs. Bott kindly. "I can't play with you to-day. I've got other things to do. Anyway, I don't approve of games like that. They're cruel."

"It's not a game," said William. "It's true. He's bein' torchered."

"I don't object to children having their little fancies and imaginings," went on Mrs. Bott, "but you ought to try and think of something pretty, William. Can't you imagine fairies and pretty fairy adventures with flowers and elves and such-like, instead of things like torchurers?"

*"Whatever mischief have you been in now,
William?" said Mrs. Bott.*

"I tell you it's Mr. Bott," shouted William excitedly. "Won't you *listen*? It's Mr. Bott who's bein' torchered."

"Now, William, don't talk nonsense," said Mrs. Bott sharply. "You ought to know at your age how wrong it is to tell stories. I *know* that Mr. Bott's in Scotland, because I had a picture post card from him this morning."

"I don't care. He *is* bein' torchered," persisted William. "I've seen him to-day through a window. In a house jus' the other side of Marleigh. He was lyin' on a table, an' a big man was pullin' his arms an' legs out of their sockets."

Mrs. Bott looked at him. There was no doubting his sincerity. Beneath its coating of garden soil his face fairly radiated earnestness. She blinked at him helplessly. Her expression registered a mixture of incredulity and apprehension.

"You—you've made a mistake, William," she said faintly. "It—it can't be Mr. Bott."

"I tell you it *is*," said William vehemently. "I know him, an' I've *seen* him bein' torchered. On a table an' his arms an' legs bein' pulled out. I tell you I know. They kidnapped him on his way to Scotland."

Mrs. Bott began to wring her plump hands.

"Oh dear," she said, "oh dear, oh dear . . . It can't be true off the pictures. Not a thing like this. I can't believe it. William," suddenly becoming stern, "it's very wrong indeed of you to try to frighten me by ridiculous tales like this. Tales that couldn't possibly be true. I'm not at all sure that I won't write and complain to your father about you. Go home at once

45

and wash your face and brush your hair and tidy yourself up. I never saw such a sight as you look."

"Well, I got like this tryin' to rescue him," pleaded William passionately. "Won't you come an' *see*, anyway?"

There was something very impressive in William's tone and expression. Mrs. Bott raised her hand to her head.

"It's the sort of thing one dreams of after lobster mayonnaise," she said faintly. "I can't believe it, William. It's impossible. I mean—well, if a thing's impossible, it's impossible, isn't it? I'll show you the picture post card I had from him this morning. It's got Highland cattle on. Ever so pretty. He'd never have sent it if he'd been kidnapped."

"Well, won't you jus' come an' *see*?" said William again.

Mrs. Bott put her hand on the bell.

"Now if I find you've been making all this up, William," she said, "I'll go *straight* to your father."

In a few minutes Mrs. Bott and William were speeding along the road in Mrs. Bott's Rolls-Royce. They looked an odd couple. William's collar and tie were still at unconventional angles. His face was still adorned with garden soil, his dishevelled hair (despite the butler's attention) with laurel leaves. Mrs. Bott, who was now in a highly emotional state, had put on her large be-feathered hat anyhow. Her face was flushed, her eyes protruded.

"We'd better stop here," said William, when the car had reached the beginning of the bottle-crowned

46

wall. "If you drive right up, it'll put them on their guard an' they'll hide him . . ."

Mrs. Bott showed every symptom of going into hysterics, then, realising that there was no suitable audience, mastered herself.

"Now, William," she said, "if I find he's not here, I'll never forgive you. No, I don't mean that, but—I mean I'll never forgive you for this awful half-hour you've given me. I'll go straight and tell your father."

"He's here all right," said William, stepping out of the car. "You come with me."

Mrs. Bott followed him to the door in the wall. Cautiously he opened it. The kitchen garden was empty. He led the way to the hedge, then across the lawn to the house.

"Now we'll look in the windows," he whispered, "an' I bet we'll soon see him bein' torchered."

Keeping well within the shelter of the bushes, they looked at the elegantly appointed drawing-room and the elegantly appointed dining-room, but saw no signs of Mr. Bott. In the next room, however, a man lay upon the table, and the man in the white coat stood by him, pulling his arms and legs in the same ungentle fashion as William had seen him pulling Mr. Bott's.

"There," he said, "didn't I tell you?"

"But that's not him," said Mrs. Bott, again wavering upon the verge of hysterics, "that's not my Botty."

"No, but it *shows*, doesn't it?" said William.

He led her to the next window, a long French window, and there upon a sort of slab they saw—unmistakably—Mr. Bott, practically naked, being pummelled unmercifully by an enormous giant of a man. His face was twisted into agonised contortions. Faint groans reached the watching pair. Immediately a tornado burst into the room. Mrs. Bott flung herself through the French window and upon the pummelling giant, beating at him with her fists and screaming: "You leave my Botty alone, you great big bully, you!"

Pandemonium followed, and William flung himself zestfully into the mêlée, hitting out right and left.

The man in the white coat appeared, and Mrs. Bott at once left the giant and attacked him. Her strength, however, had spent itself upon the giant, and her attack upon the white-coated man was lacking in verve. Comparative order gradually ensued. Mr. Bott lay on the floor, propped up against a wall; Mrs. Bott, her hair falling about her face, knelt beside him, panting.

"Oh, Botty," sobbed Mrs. Bott, "have they killed you?"

"Nearly," said Mr. Bott with a groan.

"Madam——" began the man in the white coat, but Mrs. Bott cut him short angrily.

"Don't you dare speak to me. I've got the house surrounded by aeroplanes and armoured cars, so you might as well surrender." Then, turning to her husband: "Oh, Botty, how did you come to this awful place? Did they kidnap you on the way to Scotland?"

"No," said Mr. Bott faintly, "I came—I came here for treatment."

"For what?" said his wife.

"For treatment, my dear. You know how you've

48

often said you'd like me to get my weight down. Well, I heard they did it for you here, and I wanted it to be a little surprise. I—well, my dear, I meant it to be a little birthday present for you."

"But what *is* this place?" said Mrs. Bott hysterically.

The giant had gone, and the man in the white coat stood leaning against the mantelpiece and watching them with an expression of aloof disdain. William was eagerly examining the appointments of the room. He thought that it would be useful to him in his career at Scotland Yard to know exactly what a torturer's den look like. He had just decided that a reading stand that happened to be standing in a corner was a particularly ingenious thumb-screw.

"It's a Nature Cure place," said Mr. Bott. "They do osty-something-or-other and massage and diet. Oh, my dear"—he groaned again—"the diet!"

"What diet, dear?" said Mrs. Bott solicitously.

"Starvation," groaned Mr. Bott. "They call it diet, but it's starvation. *Starvation*, pure and simple. For three days—for three—whole—days I had nothing but orange juice."

"Botty!" screamed Mrs. Bott, in sympathetic anguish. "Oh, *Botty!*"

"Nothing but orange juice," repeated Mr. Bott, dwelling with morbid relish on his harrowing experiences; "not a crumb of solid food—not one single crumb; nothing but orange juice for three—whole—days. I've never felt so empty in my life. I simply can't describe the feeling, my love. A sort of hollow ache."

"Oh, Botty!" sobbed his sorrowing wife.

"Then after those three days I began to have solid food," went on the sufferer, "but—oh, my dear, you'd hardly call it food. Raisins for breakfast! Just *Raisins!* And they won't even let me eat as many as I like of them. And raw carrots for dinner. Just imagine! Raw carrots! Then all this banging and pulling about. I can't *tell* you what I've been through."

"Oh, Botty, why didn't you let me *know*?"

"I meant it as a surprise for you, love. I wanted it to be a birthday present—me coming home with my figure back. They told me that they could take off a stone a fortnight at these places. So I only pretended to go to Scotland, and I sent some post cards to James there to send to you, so that you'd think I'd gone."

"Oh, Botty, how you must have *suffered*."

"Well, I *have* suffered, love. I won't deny it . . . but I was doing it for your sake. I thought it would be such a nice surprise for you."

Mrs. Bott clung to him in tempestuous affection.

"Oh, Botty! I don't want you any different. I don't reelly. I'll never bother you any more to get your weight down. Oh, I can't bear to think what you've been through."

She turned with a suddenly assumed hauteur to the man in the white coat, who still leant nonchalantly against the mantelpiece.

"You must release my husband at once," she said, "or I'll summon the police."

The man in the white coat smiled.

"You seem to have an entirely mistaken conception of the situation, madam," he said. "Your husband

50

*"To think that if it hadn't been for this dear boy
I shouldn't have known anything about it," said
Mrs. Bott.*

applied for admission to this establishment and has been at liberty to depart from it every moment since he entered it. Personally, I shall view his departure with equanimity. I have realised for some time that he is not likely to reflect any credit upon it. He never goes out for his prescribed walk without stopping at every other shop to guzzle cream buns—a proceeding, I need hardly say, that is forbidden by our rules."

"It's a lie," said Mr. Bott, but he avoided the eyes of the man in the white coat as he said it, and his expression spoke unmistakably of guilt.

"Well, if he did, I'm glad," said Mrs. Bott pugnaciously. "It's probably the only thing that's kept him alive. He'd be dead by now if he hadn't done . . ."

She looked round and suddenly realised William's presence. He was engaged in taking to pieces a clock that he suspected of being an elaborately contrived instrument of torture. A cut he had received from one of the smaller wheels had almost justified his suspicions. The reading stand, reduced to its component parts, lay in the middle of the floor.

"Your young friend's activities," said the man in the white coat pleasantly, "will be added to the bill."

Mrs. Bott turned to William with outstretched arms.

"To think that if it hadn't been for this dear boy I shouldn't have known anything about it. I shall always believe that he saved your life, Botty." She pressed William's reluctant head against her large, soft, perfumed bosom. "I shall never forget what I owe to you, dear boy. Never, never, never."

William walked slowly homeward. He had decided not to run away to sea. He had decided not even to go to Scotland Yard. He had come to the conclusion that as thrilling adventures can be found on one's own door-step as anywhere. In one evening he had laid bare a dastardly plot to starve and torture a respectable inhabitant of his native village, and by his quickness and resource had assured the rescue of that citizen. He remembered Mrs. Bott's words—"I shall never forget what I owe to you, dear boy. Never, never, never." The utmost possible must be made of the promise contained in her words. William's brain was already at work devising how much could be made of it, and how long her mood of gratitude could be counted on to last. Certainly this was no moment to be running away from home. There was a smile of happy anticipation on his lips as he walked along . . .

CHAPTER III

MISTAKES WILL HAPPEN

RELATIONS between Robert and William were very strained, and William was rather troubled by the fact. At an ordinary time it would not have troubled him—it was indeed a natural and usual state of affairs—but it was not an ordinary time. It was a momentous and important time. It was the week before William's birthday, and William knew that Robert, if annoyed, was quite capable of letting the day pass without any tangible tribute to it. It had happened before, and William knew that, unless Robert's wrath were assuaged, it would happen again. There was perhaps reason for Robert's wrath. Even William admitted that . . .

Robert had been acting in a dramatic entertainment organised by the local football club. The play was a thriller of a highly complicated sort, freely interspersed with screams and pistol shots and mysterious failures of the electric lights. Every character in it who tried to telephone found the cord cut, and whenever the electric lights did function, shadows of strange, bat-like figures were seen passing to and fro outside the window—a phenomenon that remained unexplained throughout the play.

The culminating moment of horror, however, was when a curtain covering a recess was withdrawn and Robert was discovered hanging head downwards on a chair, his shirt front drenched in red ink. The moment was led up to very dramatically . . . The whole of the cast gathered round the curtain, obviously in a state of extreme apprehension. One and then another approached the curtain as if to withdraw it, then shrank back, registering terror by both gesture and expression. Finally one brave spirit pulled the curtain and to the accompaniment of screams and groans discovered Robert upside-down, bathed in red ink. The heroine and her sister fainted—a sofa and easy chair being put on the stage specially to receive them—and then the curtain dropped and brought Act II to an end. Robert did not appear in this act till its culminating moment, and he naturally did not wish to spend the half-hour or so before the culminating moment upside-down, bathed in ink, or even sitting cramped in a tiny chair between the drawn curtain and a French window that was apt to collapse at a touch. Moreover, he was in charge of the refreshments, and this half-hour gave him a chance to superintend the preparation of the coffee and sandwiches that were served to the audience after the play. He therefore engaged William (at a fee of a penny each time) to sit on the chair behind the curtain till the moment of the *dénouement* approached, and then come and warn him in time for him to take his place upside-down with his head touching the floor.

William's cue for fetching Robert was "My God, what's behind that curtain?" said in a shrill falsetto (meant to express extreme terror) by Dorita Merton, a girl with very golden hair and very blue eyes, who was Robert's latest flame.

This went off very well at the rehearsals and at the first performance. William listened intently for his cue and fetched Robert at the right moment, in good time to be discovered upside-down, drenched in red ink, to the acompaniment of the shrieks and groans of the whole cast.

It was on the second and last performance that the fiasco occurred. The novelty had worn off the situation, and William was growing rather tired of it. Moreover, he was haunted by a terrible suspicion that if he had held out Robert might have increased his fee to twopence.

He had now heard the play six times and he was beginning to think that he could have written a much better one himself. Still—he fully intended to carry out his bargain and on the second night he settled himself comfortably in the arm-chair behind the curtain with an orange and a volume of the latest adventures of Sexton Blake.

William afterwards affirmed that Dorita Merton never said "My God, what's behind that curtain?" He said that if she had said it he couldn't possibly have missed it. Some members of the cast agreed that Dorita had omitted it, but others said that she had not. They said that they remembered hearing her say it quite distinctly. And anyway, they added, that was no excuse for William, because he ought to have been following the play carefully behind his curtain and have known that it was time to fetch

Robert whether Dorita said "My God, what's behind that curtain?" or not.

Whatever the rights and wrongs of the case, the fact remains that when the curtain was withdrawn, in the carefully worked up atmosphere of horror and mystery, all that could be seen was a small boy in a tweed suit, leaning back comfortably in an arm-chair, eating an orange with considerable gusto and reading a novelette. This sight seemed hardly sufficient to account for the screams and shrieks of terror with which the actors—continuing to play their parts with true British doggedness—greeted it.

Robert, of course, was furious. The second night audience was much more important than the first night audience. All the officials of the football club were there. All Dorita's relations and his own were there. Everybody who was anybody was there, and William, said Robert, had disgraced him—Robert— for ever. Never again, he said, would he hold up his head. His whole life was ruined. Nothing awaited him but a dishonoured old age brought upon him prematurely by William. Nobody, said Robert, would ever talk about anything else for the rest of his life. They'd all tell other people and the other people would tell other people till the news had spread all over England, till he couldn't go anywhere in the whole world where people weren't laughing at him. It was no use doing anything at all with his life now. It was ruined. Absolutely ruined. Even if he invented anything or was made Prime Minister people would only laugh at him now after this.

William bore this tirade with comparative meekness,

only persisting to affirm that Dorita had not said "My God, what's behind that curtain?"

It was Dorita, of course, who gave the situation its peculiar bitterness. For Dorita, too, considered herself disgraced for ever by William's unfortunate mistake and, most unfairly, blamed Robert for it.

"I'd invited every friend I'd got in the world to it," she lamented; "and I'd invited a friend of my uncle's who knows a man who knows Cochran's cousin, and I was sure it would lead to something, because everyone says I have a talent for acting and I know I have myself, and it's just a question of people like Cochran hearing about you, and now my uncle's friend just goes into roars of laughter whenever anyone mentions the wretched play, and, if Cochran does hear about it, it will be just as a joke, and it's perhaps the only chance I'll ever have all my life of getting famous and all spoilt through you."

"Through me?" said Robert indignantly. "You mean through William. And you couldn't possibly feel worse about it than I do . . ."

"Oh, couldn't I?" said Dorita. "How do you know I couldn't, considering you don't know what I feel. I can't think why you ever let him sit there like that. Anyone with any real feeling for acting would have wanted to *act* the part, not sneak out of it half the time you did."

"Do you mean I ought to have hung down from a chair like that with my head on the floor for half an hour?" said Robert.

"Why not?" said Dorita. "Any *real* actor would have."

58

"I'd be dead if I'd done that," said Robert.

Dorita gave a sniff, implying that that would not have been any great calamity.

But gradually another subject replaced the play fiasco in Dorita's mind. It was a series of Shakespearian tableaux that was being given by the school which both William and her own small brother attended.

"They're doing a scene from King John," she said, "and I do hope they choose Georgie to be Arthur. He's such a dear little boy. Just the type for it, you know. *Ever* so sweet. There's some talk of them choosing his cousin, who's in the same form and who's a perfectly hateful little boy. We shall all be most *terribly* upset if they choose his cousin. I don't really mind them not choosing either, but if they choose Georgie's cousin instead of Georgie, I shall simply die. We'll all simply die."

Robert, relieved that she had ceased to harp upon the unfortunate episode of the play, expressed interest and sympathy.

"I'm sure they'll choose your brother," he said.

"You'll do what you can about it, anyway, won't you," she pleaded, "because Georgie's such a *sweet* little boy?"

"Er—yes," he said, "I'll certainly do what I can. But I'm afraid I can't do much. You see, I'm not connected with the school in any way."

"But your brother goes there," she said.

"Y-yes," he admitted. "He does go there, but—he hasn't actually got much influence there."

"Yes, but he *might* be able to do something, mightn't he?"

59

Robert admitted very doubtfully that perhaps he might . . .

The next day, however, it turned out that another boy, by name Herbert Frances, had been chosen to play Arthur. Dorita, whose entire interest was now concentrated upon the affair, rang up Robert to tell him about him.

"Of course, I feel dreadful in a *way*," she said earnestly, "because this boy they've chosen isn't *half* as sweet as Georgie, but—well, of course, I'd feel *much* worse if they'd chosen his cousin, because my aunt's very silly and seems to think that he's cleverer than Georgie, and really Georgie's heaps the cleverest of the two."

Robert was beginning to tire of the subject of Georgie, but he was grateful to it for ousting the subject of the play, and he was as much enthralled as ever by the very golden hair and very blue eyes of Dorita.

Now that the question of Georgie appeared to be settled, Robert again began to try to lead the interest of the beloved into more congenial regions—regions of dances and motor runs and pictures and *tête-à-tête* in general. Dorita was showing every sign of being willing to have her interest led into these regions and all was merry as a marriage bell when suddenly the Georgie question popped up again.

When Robert called for the beloved one afternoon he found her pale and distraught.

"That boy who was going to be Arthur has got a dreadful cold," she said, "and if it doesn't get well before the day he can't possibly be in it. And they say that it's between Georgie and his cousin again. Oh *dear*, it's so trying. I thought it was all settled. I tell you if they choose Georgie's cousin I shall *die*. *Literally* die. Georgie's so sweet and his cousin's the most *hateful* little wretch."

Robert tried again to whip up interest in the Georgie-Arthur question.

"Oh, they'll choose Georgie," he said. "I'm sure they'll choose Georgie."

"But *will* they?" said Dorita gloomily. "People are so *unfair*, you know. And Georgie *is* so sweet. He honestly is. We *all* think so."

In vain Robert tried to lead her attention back to dances and motor rides and cinemas and *tête à tête* in general. It refused to leave Georgie. The day of the entertainment drew nearer, and Herbert's cold—despite the attentions of his whole family, who poured out upon him in an unending stream every remedy for a cold that was suggested to them by a large and interested circle of friends—grew no better. His nose and eyes continued to be a fiery red, he continued to sneeze incessantly and to assure everyone at frequent intervals, but more and more indistinctly each time, that he was "a liddle better dow, thag you."

Dorita's excitement rose to fever pitch.

"I know that boy's not going to be fit to do Arthur," she assured Robert; "and if they don't choose Georgie I don't know what I shall do. I don't talk much about it," she added, "because I'm one of those people who feel things very deeply, but don't say much. I'm very reserved, you know . . . Of course, it's the thought of Georgie's cousin that really worries me. I may not

61

have said much about it"—Robert gasped, then quickly changed his gasp to a cough—"but it's in my mind all the time and——" She looked at him reflectively. "Do you know, if this boy's cold *is* too bad for him to be Arthur on the day and they choose Georgie's cousin instead of Georgie, I shall really begin to feel that you've brought me bad luck, because nothing's really gone right with me since that wretched play."

This remark made Robert, on his side, deeply thoughtful. He gathered from it that if Georgie were not chosen as Arthur his chances of continuing to be Dorita's favoured escort were pretty slender.

That evening he cautiously sounded William. William, however, was not responsive. He professed an utter indifference to the doings of the preparatory department of his school. He did not know Herbert Frances, he did not know Georgie, he did not know Georgie's cousin. He did not, moreover, want to know them. He knew nothing about the tableaux, and he had no intention of demeaning himself so far as to attend the performance. His attitude made Robert still more thoughtful. On the evening before the performance he approached William casually and said:

"Oh, by the way, William, it's your birthday next week, isn't it?"

William agreed that it was. There was a faint gleam of hope in his eye.

"What would you like for a present?" continued Robert. William considered this question in silence for a moment. He could hardly believe that Robert really intended to give him a present after the affair of the play, and he was aware that to mention something too expensive would prejudice his chances of getting anything at all.

"Well," he said modestly, "I'd like any little thing . . . I've had my mouth organ took off me in school by old Stinks and he won't give it me back."

"Of course," said Robert loftily, "you must expect that sort of thing if you make a nuisance of yourself . . . but I may possibly get you another. I won't say I will. It all depends on how you behave between now and your birthday . . . By the way, with regard to those theatricals at your school, I hear that there's every possibility that Herbert Whoever-he-is won't be able to take the part of Arthur and that it will lie between Georgie Merton and his cousin. Personally, of course, I hope that Georgie Merton will have the part, because I believe that he'd be much more suitable."

Then Robert walked away, leaving William sunk in thought. William, of course, fully understood the trend of Robert's remarks. If he could somehow or other bring it about that Georgie Merton and not his cousin should take the place of Herbert in the preparatory department's tableaux, then Robert would give him a mouth organ as a reward.

That afternoon after school he walked through the playground of the preparatory department, in order to take a brief survey of its inhabitants and discover if possible which of them was Georgie Merton. He walked through in ostentatious aloofness, examining the sky above him or the ground beneath him, scorning to appear to be taking any interest in the doings of

the inferior mortals around him. But, despite his pretended absorption, he sent quick glances of enquiry
to right and left as he passed on his way. Suddenly he
came upon two small boys fighting. The smaller one
was fighting gamely and in accordance with the rules
of fair play. The other one was kicking and punching
wildly and yet was getting the worst of it. William
took to the smaller one at once. He had a merry,
impudent, freckled face and a twinkle in his eyes.
William felt instinctively that, despite his youth, he was
the right sort of person to be wrecked on a desert
island with. That was William's unvarying criterion of
character. If a new acquaintance did not strike William
as the right sort of person to be wrecked on a desert
island with, then William had no further use for him,
whatever his other talents and accomplishments.

The other boy had a mop of auburn curls and long,
effeminate eyelashes. He was fat and flabby and pale,
and looked furtive and bad-tempered. Old ladies
would probably have raved over his curls and long
lashes, thought William, in a lightning summing up of
his character, but on a desert island he would be worse
than useless.

"Here!" said William to him sternly, "can't you
fight properly without kicking?"

He looked at William open-mouthed, then turned
and fled with a howl of terror. The other boy gave
William a friendly grin.

"What's your name?" said William.

"George Merton," said the boy.

"And who's the other boy?"

"My cousin," said George. "He and I hate each

other. We fight every day. He kicks like that because he can't beat me unless he does."

"I thought you were fighting jolly well," said William approvingly, and passed on his way

He felt much cheered and encouraged. George Merton was a boy after his own heart. It would be a welcome task to assure that he and not the obnoxious cousin should play Arthur. William, of course, had no idea how to set about this. He decided that the only thing to do at present was to hover near the preparatory department to catch such news as leaked out from it.

The news that leaked out that night was that Herbert's mother was certain that he would be quite well enough to play Arthur by to-morrow. She had bought a new medicine that was guaranteed to cure a cold in one night and she was giving Herbert a double dose to make quite sure.

William, going away with this news, came upon George Merton looking for caterpillars in the hedge. They conversed for a few minutes and discovered many tastes and ideals in common. George, too, disliked civilisation and had decided to discover and reign over a hitherto undiscovered island when he was grown up.

"An' I'm not goin' to have people washin' and brushin' their hair an' bein' polite all day in *my* country," he said firmly; "there's goin' to be a law against it."

"That's a jolly good idea," agreed William, and added: "Do you want to be Arthur of whatever he is in this ole tableaux if Herbert can't be it?"

C

George grinned.

"I wouldn't for myself," he said, "only if I'm not it my cousin will be, an' he'll crow over me for all he's worth. They're always goin' on at me, sayin' why don't I keep myself clean an' tidy like what he does, so it'll be jolly well snooks for them if they choose me for the ole tableaux an' not him. But anyway Herbert's mother says that he'll be well enough."

"I hope he won't," said William, who was now beginning to feel that that would be too tame an ending to the affair.

The next morning, however, he heard that Herbert's mother had written to say that she was keeping Herbert in bed for the morning and giving him another double dose of the new cure, and that she was quite sure he would be well enough to take the part of Arthur in the afternoon. Still—William liked to be prepared for anything and the evening before he had made a thorough investigation of the precincts of the preparatory department and had laid certain nebulous plans that would depend entirely on circumstances.

The whole school was given a holiday on the afternoon of the performance, and William at once repaired to the preparatory department to see how affairs were going on. All was confusion and pandemonium. Herbert's mother had rung up to say that the new cold cure had upset Herbert's stomach so much that she was afraid that he couldn't possibly come. He'd been sick all morning and was in the process of being sick again. She added that both she and Herbert were bitterly disappointed and that she hoped they would return the money she had paid for her ticket . . .

A master came out into the playground holding a velvet doublet in his hand. His face wore a desperate and harassed expression. He looked round the seething mass of small boys . . . then his eye fell on William and he brightened. William's purposeful air gave him for the moment a misleading appearance of earnestness and virtue.

"Oh, I say, you!" he called. "Will you fetch me—well, I don't suppose you know any of their names, do you?—but you can't mistake this kid. He's the only kid in the place with red curls. Red curls. Find a kid with red curls for me and tell him to come and get into Arthur's togs at once as the other brat's laid up. I don't see him in the playground, but he may be in the shrubbery. Red curls. You can't mistake him."

William hastened into the shrubbery and there he found the two cousins engaging in their daily fight. The owner of the red curls had just landed a masterly kick in his opponent's stomach. William laid a hand on the red curls and dragged their owner unceremoniously away.

"You're wanted," he said tersely.

"Who wants me?" said the youth, wriggling against William's relentless grip.

"They want you to be Arthur. Come on. I'll show you the way to the dressing-room."

"Ha, ha!" jeered the youth triumphantly. "An' that ole Georgie said they'd choose him. I told him they'd never choose *his* ugly mug and I was right, wasn't I?"

"Come on and don't talk so much," said William shortly, drawing the red head firmly towards a coal-shed that stood in the farthest corner of the shrubbery.

"This isn't the way to the dressing-room," protested the youth."

"Yes it is," said William, "they've changed it to here." He opened the door. "Here it is."

"That's a coal-shed," objected his victim.

But he had entered it in order to make sure that it really was a coal-shed, and in that second William slammed the door and thrust the latch home. Angry shouts arose at once from within, but they were drowned by the pandemonium from the playground.

William returned to the other end of the shrubbery and found the other small boy engaged in his search for caterpillars.

"I say," he greeted William, "I believe this is an elephant hawk. Is it an elephant hawk? Look at it."

"You've got to come with me," said William, "you're wanted."

He drew him back to the playground and left him in the middle of it, saying: "Stay here."

Then he approached the door where the master still stood gazing round despairingly, dangling the velvet doublet.

"I can't find anyone with red curls," said William unblushingly. "That boy was in the shrubbery"— pointing to Georgie who still stood where William had left him—"but he's not the one, is he?"

The master looked at him and brightened.

"He'll do," he said. "He was in the running. We tossed up which to have and it came to the other, but this one will do just as well. Tell him to come to me at once."

William delivered his message, and George, first handing his possible elephant hawk into William's care, went to the door and was hustled out of sight by the master.

William waited outside the main entrance. Pandemonium ceased in the playground and the preparatory department fled into the hall to take their seats. The first members of the audience began to arrive. Robert and Dorita arrived together. William winked and nodded to Robert in order to inform him that all was well. He must make it quite clear to Robert afterwards that he had to run tremendous risks and exercise superhuman cunning in order to bring about this happy consummation. A mouth organ, after all, was very inadequate remuneration. He'd tell Robert that he wanted a camera instead. A *good* camera. Or perhaps it would be best to put the whole thing upon a cash basis. Ten shillings surely wouldn't be too much to ask for a thing like this. Ten shillings at least . . .

The doors were shut and the performance was beginning. William, who had never intended to pay an entrance fee, hoisted himself up with some difficulty to one of the windows that gave him a partial view of the stage. The tableaux succeeded each other to the accompaniment of hysterical applause from the actors' aunts and sisters and mothers and nurses, who formed the audience.

Then came the tableaux from King John with George in a black velvet suit and lace collar. William, craning his neck to see Dorita and Robert, threw them a proud and self-congratulatory glance. But Dorita appeared to have been suddenly taken ill. Her eyes bulged, her face went red. She rose and, with a wild glance around, plunged out of the building, followed by the bewildered Robert. She was probably overcome by sheer joy, thought William, dropping from his perch. He must show her the rest of his efforts on his behalf. She must be made to realise what masterly strategy he had displayed. She, too, might feel impelled to place the matter on a cash basis. Ten shillings from Robert and ten shillings from her . . . It sounded too good to be true, but such things had been known to happen. William himself had once met an actual living boy who had been given a pound by a complete stranger for finding her lost ring. And, even if they couldn't rise to it, he'd still have the mouth organ . . . He played on an imaginary mouth organ as he waited for them.

They were coming out of the building now.

"I shall never forgive you," Dorita was saying hysterically. "You told me that Georgie had got the part—you *told* me so . . ."

"Yes, but—but——" began the bewildered Robert.

William had hastened down to the coal-shed. She'd be jolly grateful to him when she saw what he'd done for her. He unlatched the door and the red-haired child came out, howling angrily. But he was red-haired no longer. His attempts to escape from his prison had covered him with coal-dust from head to foot. He was a terrible and sinister object—black and howling. He fled from his prison round the side of

70

the school and straight into Dorita's arms. She screamed wildly.

"Georgie! Oh, *Georgie*! What have they *done* to you?"

"That's not Georgie," explained William patiently, "Georgie's in there actin'. It was me that got him in. An' I got his cousin shut in the coal-shed so's they'd be sure to choose your brother . . ."

"My brother!" shrieked Dorita, hugging the black-encrusted form to her bosom. "*This* is my brother."

"That boy shut me in the coal-shed," howled the child, pointing to William. "Why doesn't somebody *do* something to him for shutting me in the coal-shed?"

"B-b-but the other one said he was called George Merton," stammered William.

"They're *both* called George Merton," screamed Dorita. "You *must* have known they were both called George Merton."

William realised suddenly that he had never even asked the name of the red-headed one. He had been simply George Merton's cousin.

He realised, too, that the situation was past hope and looked round desperately for escape.

"Why doesn't someone *do* something to that boy for shutting me in the coal-shed?" howled the black one again vociferously.

But he was a little less black than he had been before, as he had rubbed a good deal of his coal off on to his sister's pale fawn costume, which she was wearing to-day for the first time. She noticed this suddenly and hurled Georgie from her with horror and disgust.

"Get away," she sobbed in fury, "you hateful, dirty little boy!"

She tore open her bag and glanced at her reflection in her mirror. Her worst suspicions were confirmed. The side of her face that she had rested in sisterly emotion upon Georgie's curls was adorned by a bold smudge of black. Her once white gloves were black. A small piece of coal adhered to her golden hair.

"*Oh!*" she screamed, then with a stamp of her foot, "I shall never speak to any of you again. Never, never, *never!*" Livid with fury beneath her coal-dust, she swung round upon Robert.

"As for you——!"

Robert at bay swung round upon William.

"As for *you*——!"

But William was not there. He was already nearly a quarter of a mile off.

He threw an imaginary mouth organ away from him as he ran.

CHAPTER IV

WILLIAM AND CLEOPATRA

WILLIAM was feeling slightly depressed. He had had a run of bad luck that had culminated in his breaking Miss Hathaway's garden frame by falling into it from the high wall that ran round her garden. High walls always had a fascination for William, especially if they were narrow as well as high. He liked to see how far and how quickly he could walk along them. A tree grew temptingly near this particular wall, and William had climbed the tree, hoisted himself upon the wall and, balancing with outstretched arms, had begun to walk along it. The top had been level, and William had progressed at a pace of which he had been very proud till, yielding to over-confidence, he had attempted to run and had descended heavily into Miss Hathaway's garden frame. Had it not happened that Miss Hathaway was in her greenhouse at the time William might have escaped unnoticed, but as it was, he rose from the bed of the frame to confront an enraged Miss Hathaway, who pointed a watering-can at him accusingly and said:

"Now I've caught you, William Brown. And it's not the first time you've damaged my garden either."

William removed a seedling from his mouth and considered the situation thoughtfully. There had been a recent occasion when he had taken a short cut through Miss Hathaway's garden in order to intercept one of his enemies and, tripping up at an inopportune moment, had fallen into the middle of one of Miss Hathaway's flower-beds, crushing several choice plants in his descent. He had hoped that the incident was unobserved but evidently it had not been. There was one redeeming feature of the present situation, and that was that his father was away and so she could not at any rate complain to him. Her next words, however, destroyed his feeling of security on this score.

"I know your father's away," she said, "but he's coming back on Friday and first thing on Saturday morning I'm going to tell him."

Her expression was grim and unrelenting.

"But, listen," pleaded William eagerly, "just listen . . ."

She raised her hand in a majestic gesture.

"Not another *word*, William," she said, and, turning on her heel, walked with great dignity into the house.

William bound up a cut knee with a grimy handkerchief, removed some more seedlings from his hair and mouth, and set off slowly homewards. His face, beneath its coating of prepared potting soil, was very thoughtful. His birthday was the Sunday after his father's return, and Mr. Brown had promised to give him ten shillings for his birthday present on condition that he had a good report of his conduct during his absence. William knew that, with the well-known and universal meanness of grown-ups, he would be only too ready to take advantage of Miss Hathaway's complaint and refuse to give William any money at all.

There were only two days before his return. Miss Hathaway's expression had been the expression of one not to be moved from her determination by either reasoning or entreaty. During lunch his mother asked him anxiously why he was so quiet. He replied darkly that he'd jolly well got enough to make anyone quiet, and relapsed into gloomy silence.

After lunch he went upstairs and spent an hour not only removing all traces of his descent into the garden frame but also putting an added lustre upon his appearance that was little short of startling. He scrubbed his knees till they were sore, he cleaned his nails, he washed his face with pumice-stone to be on the safe side, he "borrowed" Robert's hair oil to stick down his hair, he put on his Sunday suit and a clean collar and tie. Thus resplendent and wearing his most innocent and appealing expression, he set off in the direction of Miss Hathaway's house. He felt hopefully that his appearance should go far to remove the unfortunate impression caused by the morning's escapade. He practised his "polite voice" as he walked along the road, apologising profusely to the hedges on either side of him for having broken their garden frame, stopping earnestly to assure a straying cow that he would repair the damage himself with glue so that it would be even better than new . . . Soaring to yet higher flights of eloquence and invention he informed a hen crossing the road that he had only climbed the wall because he thought that he had heard a cry for help. It was in fact his eagerness to come to her rescue that had made him fall down upon her garden frame. His spirits rose higher as he neared Miss Hathaway's house. He felt that no one—not even Miss Hathaway herself—could resist such an appeal as he was going to make. By the time he had reached her front door he had fully persuaded himself that he had really climbed the wall in reply to a cry of help, and his expression was an impressive blend of injured innocence and wistful appeal.

The housemaid who opened the door seemed—rather to his chagrin—unmoved by his appearance and expression.

"She doesn't want to see you," she said, and shut the door unceremoniously in his face.

William felt disconcerted by this unexpected turn of events.

He was firmly convinced, however, that Miss Hathaway, once she had heard his story, would not only pardon him but feel actually grateful to him (he was becoming more and more certain that he had heard that cry for help). It was simply a question of persuading her to listen to him. He rang the bell again with great vehemence. The housemaid opened the door, also with great vehemence.

"You be off this minute," she said angrily, "or I'll box your ears."

So ready did she look to fulfil her threat that William flung dignity to the winds and fled precipitately down to the garden gate. In the road he stood throwing stones absently over the hedge and brooding disconsolately on the unfairness of life. All this trouble

"*You be off this minute,*" said the housemaid
angrily, "*or I'll box your ears.*"

for nothing, making himself *raw* with cleanness and all for nothing . . . She wouldn't even listen to him . . . all that fuss about an old garden frame that he'd only broken with trying to come to her rescue . . . it was jolly unfair. A larger stone than usual, despatched over the hedge with a force born of bitterness and disappointment, hit Farmer Jenks, who happened to be crossing the field, neatly on the ear. With a cry of pain and rage Farmer Jenks leapt the stile between the field and the road, and, seeing his old enemy, William, started off in pursuit. William led him zestfully into a neighbouring wood and there let him come almost to grips with him several times before adroitly evading his grasp by dodging round a tree. He finally threw him off by following a stream along its narrow bed under the roadway, and returned home much exhilarated but with his pristine spruceness sadly dimmed.

Thinking over the affair of the garden frame, he was now firmly convinced that Miss Hathaway's housemaid was his enemy and that out of sheer malice she had not even told Miss Hathaway of his visit. Generally speaking, William was not popular with the domestic staffs of his neighbours. They classed him with tramps and gypsies, and showed him as scant courtesy. Yes, the more he thought of it the more convinced he became that it was Miss Hathaway's maid who had denied him admittance, not Miss Hathaway herself. "Frightened prob'ly I'd tread on a carpet or touch somethin'," he said bitterly to himself. "They seem to think you can go about same as a ghost not treadin' anyway or touchin' anythin'."

He indulged his sense of grievance against Miss Hathaway's maid by imagining a scene in which he captured her at the head of his pirate band, and compelled her to spend the months of her imprisonment cleaning up muddy footmarks that he made purposely every morning. "That'd jolly well *teach* her," he said grimly. But this picture, though a pleasing one, did nothing actually to further the situation, and he set himself seriously to consider what must be done. After much cogitation he decided that the next step was to waylay Miss Hathaway in the village. It would be useless to approach the house again, guarded as it was by the hostile maid. He must waylay Miss Hathaway herself and put his case before her. Surely when she knew that he had only climbed the wall in order to rescue her she would see the matter in a different light . . . He hung about the village shop the next morning and soon saw Miss Hathaway approaching it on her bicycle. Outside the shop she dismounted. William approached her eagerly.

"Please, Miss Hathaway," he began, trying to preserve the exact balance between eagerness and politeness, "when I climbed your wall the other day it was because——"

She raised her hand in a commanding gesture of dismissal. "Not another *word*, William." And she passed into the shop, without looking at him.

William, feeling considerably less optimistic than he had felt a few moments before but having by no means given up hope, waited till she came out and then accosted her again.

"Please, Miss Hathaway, about me gettin' on your wall yesterday, I thought I heard——"

Again she raised her hand in the commanding gesture of dismissal.

"Not a *word*, William. I shall complain to your father immediately on his return."

"If you'll jus' *listen*, I can explain——"

But he was addressing the empty air. Miss Hathaway was already pedalling her way down the road, every inch of her thin, angular figure expressing grim resolution.

William realised that it is impossible to waylay a person who refuses to be waylaid. He lacked the optical power of the Ancient Mariner. So despondent did he feel that he even accompanied his mother meekly, and without protest, on a visit to an aunt whom he had always disliked. The aunt, after delivering her usual homily on How Much Better Children Behaved when She was Young, gave him an ancient book of engravings to look through as a great treat. He sat at the table, turning over the leaves morosely. "This is what comes to helpin' people," he said to himself bitterly. "I jolly well won't go the next time I hear her cry for help. Pinchin' all my money off me!" The picture darkened so that he almost believed that Miss Hathaway had deliberately lured him into her garden by a feigned cry for help in order to rob him of his money.

He flicked over the pages one by one, glancing contemptuously at each. Giving him a picture book to look at as if he was a kid! Then he stopped at a picture, examining it with sudden interest. It showed a woman standing on a half-unrolled carpet in front of a Roman general.

"What's this about?" he demanded.

The aunt came over to him and, adjusting her pince-nez, inspected the picture.

"That, William," she said, "is Cleopatra. Cæsar had refused to grant her an interview. So she sent him a present of a carpet, and when it was unrolled she was in the middle of it and so he had to grant her the interview. Very foolish and unsuitable. Turn on a few pages, dear, and you'll find a nice picture of shepherds tending their flocks on the hills."

But William was gazing with deepening interest at the picture of Cleopatra arising from the carpet. That was a jolly good idea. He imagined Cleopatra at the door of Cæsar's house being turned away by an indignant housemaid . . . accosting him as he descended from his bicycle outside the village shop and being unceremoniously brushed aside . . . and then this idea of a carpet. It was a jolly clever idea . . . He continued to gaze at the picture till it was time to go home. On his way home he broke a long silence by saying suddenly:

"How much do carpets cost, mother?"

"Pounds and pounds, dear," said Mrs. Brown.

"Aren't there any cheaper than that?" he demanded.

"I suppose you can get very common ones for about a pound, but it wouldn't last any time at all, of course."

"I suppose you couldn't get a very, *very* common one for about sixpence?" asked William hopefully.

"Oh, no, dear, of *course* not," said Mrs. Brown.

William abandoned the idea of the carpet. He

abandoned it reluctantly, because the mental picture of himself rising to his feet as the carpet was unrolled and confronting an amazed Miss Hathaway, like Cleopatra in the engraving, was a very pleasant one. He would have explained all about the broken garden frame and the cry for help before she recovered from her astonishment, and she would be overcome by gratitude and penitence.

The more he thought about it the more convinced of this he became. It was simply a question of getting her to listen to him. William had a great faith in his eloquence. It was a pity that carpets were so dear . . .

Though he had now given up his plan of actually making his way into Miss Hathaway's presence enveloped in a carpet, still the general idea seemed to him so good that he had not altogether abandoned it. Surely there must be something cheaper than a carpet that would serve the purpose . . .

He was ruminating the subject as he went along the road that led past the station the next morning. Suddenly he stopped. An enormous brand-new dog kennel stood there. A most magnificent dog kennel. A very palace of a dog kennel. And there was a dog in it—a friendly brown dog who pushed his nose through the bars that closed up the ornate doorway of the structure. William forgot everything else in his interest in the dog. He knelt down on the ground, playing with it and stroking it through the bars. He found a dusty fragment of biscuit in his pocket and offered it. To his immense delight the dog ate it.

"Like to come out for a run down the road?" he

said: "I bet you'd like to come out for a run down the road, wouldn't you?"

The brown dog wagged its tail so expectantly that William felt that he had definitely pledged himself to take it for a little run down the road. He examined the fastenings of the barred gate. Yes, there was a latch that slipped back, and then it opened quite easily. There couldn't be any harm in taking the little dog for a run down the road and back, and then shutting him up in the kennel again.

"Come on," he said as he opened it, "come on for a little run then."

The dog leapt out, curvetting round William's feet joyfully. Attached to his collar was a large luggage label.

"Come on," said William again, setting off at a run down the road. The dog ran on in front of him. It was rather a good runner, and William could barely keep up with it. At the bend in the road he stopped breathlessly. "Now come on back," he said.

But the dog apparently did not hear. It went on at full speed down the road.

"Hi!" shouted William. "Hi! Come back!"

The dog paid no attention. It went on running down the road.

"Hi!" shouted William again, desperately. "Hi! Come back! I'll get into a row if you don't."

This appeal failed to move the dog. It went on running down the road without even looking back. It had now disappeared round the next bend. William panted after it, but the bend showed no brown dog to him. It had vanished completely from the landscape. He struggled on to the cross-roads, but none of the four roads that met there revealed any sign of the brown dog. He walked slowly back to the dog kennel and closed the barred gate, hoping thus to postpone detection of the crime as far as possible. While doing this he caught sight suddenly of the label nailed on to the roof of the kennel: "Miss Hathaway, Laurel Cottage."

Immediately an idea struck him with such overwhelming force that for a moment he actually saw stars. A dog kennel was as good as a carpet. He would go to Miss Hathaway's in the dog kennel. Instead of arising from a carpet, he would crawl out of a dog kennel. And then, before she recovered from her paralysis of amazement, he would make her his apology and explanation. The disappearance of the rightful owner of the kennel was, of course, a slightly awkward feature of the situation, but he hoped to persuade her that it had escaped before the kennel had reached the station. He looked up and down the road. No one was in sight. Obviously the kennel had been put there by the porter to wait for the carrier's cart. Cautiously William unlatched the little barred gate. Yes, it was just large enough to allow him to squirm in. He squirmed in. There was a good deal of straw inside, and somehow not quite as much room as he had thought there would be. Still—he could curl up in it fairly comfortably. He found that there was a little wooden door that could be drawn across the aperture as well as the barred gate. Hearing the sounds of the approach of the carrier's cart

84

he hastily drew it. The kennel lurched wildly and he hit his head with great violence against the side.

"Coo!" he heard a man's voice say. "It ain't 'alf 'eavy. What's in it?"

"Porter said it were a kennel and dawg inside," said another voice.

"It ain't no dawg," said the first voice. "More like bricks by the weight of it. Bricks or coal."

"Coal," said the second voice. "Yes, I bet it's coal. A new-fangled coal-shed made in the shape of a dawg's kennel. Coo, the things they make nowadays!"

This explanation seemed to satisfy both of them, and they hoisted William up on to the cart. To William it was as if the kennel had become suddenly inspired with malignant life and were battering his head from all sides. He protected himself from it as well as he could, then cautiously opened the little wooden door in order to admit some air. The cart rattled and jolted along the road and finally stopped outside Miss Hathaway's house.

Miss Hathaway came out, a shawl wrapped round her head, and stood half-way down the garden path.

"I won't come any nearer," she called to the driver, "I've got the most dreadful cold, and I don't want to give it to anyone. That's the dog kennel, isn't it? It's for my sister's birthday present, and I meant to take it to her myself to-day in a cab, but with this awful cold I can't. Now I want you to take it on to my sister's for me—it's at Upper Marleigh—and kindly give her this note with it, will you? The address is on the envelope."

She came near enough to him to hand him the

letter at arm's length, keeping her head well turned away.

"I mustn't come near you," she said, "it's a dreadful cold."

She sneezed three times as if to prove her words, then scurried indoors.

The driver glanced at the address, said "Right 'm'," started up his horse, and set off towards Upper Marleigh.

William was quite unaware of this interlude. The jolting of the cart had so battered his head that finally he had wrapped it round in straw, completely encasing it. This made him deaf and blind to all around him, and during the interview at Miss Hathaway's he was conscious only of a blessed respite from the murderous assaults of the sides of his kennel upon him. He had no idea even that they had passed Miss Hathaway's house and were now on the way to Upper Marleigh. He thought that it was rather a long journey, but he realised that any journey taken under those particular conditions would seem long.

At last the cart came to a standstill, and he felt the kennel being lifted down—a little more gently this time—and carried along to the accompaniment of exclamations of surprise at its weight. Then it was set down with a bump that nearly dislocated his neck and he was aware of a babel of voices around him. Miss Hathaway's sister, surrounded by a large concourse of friends and relations who had come to celebrate her birthday, was reading her sister's letter aloud:

DEAR ANGELA,

I send herewith my birthday present. I had meant to bring it myself but, alas, I have a most dreadful cold. I am almost prostrate with it. Well, dear Angela, I hope you will like this kennel and its occupant. I think indeed that you will love the occupant, who is the *sweetest* thing. Please give it a kiss on the end of its nose for me. And now, dear, many happy returns of the day and much love,

From,
YOUR LOVING SISTER.

William, whose head was still encircled in straw, had heard none of this. He believed that he had at last reached Miss Hathaway's house and was preparing the speech that he must deliver as soon as he emerged from his hiding-place. He had drawn away some of the straw from his eyes so that he could see, and had opened the little wooden door and was now fumbling with the barred gate.

"Open it," said someone.

A hand came down and firmly withdrew the barred gate.

William began to crawl out.

A sudden silence fell.

They stared aghast at the straw-covered object that was slowly emerging. Even its face was shrouded in straw. It rose to its feet and, approaching Miss Hathaway's sister, who bore a strong resemblance to Miss Hathaway, began to speak in a hoarse voice:

"I came on to your garden wall 'cause I thought I heard a cry for help. That was why I came on to your garden wall. An' that was how I came to break your garden frame 'cause I was hurrying to get to you 'cause of this cry for help. An'——"

He approached nearer, gesticulating vehemently. She gave a wild scream of terror and started to the door, followed by her guests.

"The police!" she screamed. "The police, quickly!"

She fled out of the house, still followed by her terrified guests.

William unwound the straw from his head and looked about him. He was alone in a room with a large table laid for tea. Laid for a generous tea. Iced cake,

William crawled out and stood up. A sudden silence fell.

cakes composed almost wholly of layers of cream, jellies, trifles, meringues, chocolate biscuits.

William was bruised from head to foot and his mouth was full of straw, but the sight of this feast made him realise that his appetite was unimpaired. He was in fact hungrier than he had ever been in his life before. He decided just to try the trifle. He would take so little that the people wouldn't notice when they came back. He couldn't think why they'd all run off like that. The whole situation was inexplicable, and he relinquished all attempts to understand it. Instead he stared in amazement at the empty dish of trifle. Surely he hadn't eaten all that! There seemed, however, to be no other explanation of its disappearance. He considered it thoughtfully for a few moments and then took a spoonful of the jelly. It was the best jelly he had ever tasted. After some consideration he decided that now the trifle was gone it would be as well for the jelly to go too. No one ever provided jelly at a party without trifle. If there was no trifle, there might as well be no jelly. He finished it up quickly and thoroughly, and then considered the rest of the feast. He was still hungry. As he'd probably get into trouble for eating the jelly and trifle anyway, he might as well do the thing properly. He proceeded, therefore, to do the thing properly. The cake, composed chiefly of layers of cream, was a very king of cakes. William ate slice after slice of it. As his hunger was appeased so his sense of mystification increased. Where was everyone? Why had they all run away like that? Had Miss Hathaway accepted his explanation or hadn't she? A glance out of the window deep-

ened his mystification still further. For this was not
Miss Hathaway's house at all. The garden was not
Miss Hathaway's garden. The road outside this house
was not the road outside Miss Hathaway's house.

As if to sustain him against this shock, William went
back to the table and ate six meringues in quick
succession. He noticed that both table and floor were
plentifully bestrewn with straw. He picked one or
two pieces up with a vague idea of lessening the sum
total of his iniquities, then desisted and went to the
window again. All the people were returning. He
stood in the shadow of the curtain to watch them.
A policeman headed the procession. Someone in the
rear carried the brown dog who had evidently been
found and brought to Miss Hathaway. Miss Hathaway herself was there, sneezing copiously, her head
still wrapped in a shawl. Someone must have fetched
her in order to confront her with her strange birthday
gift.

The procession slowed down as it neared the door.
William could hear excited voices raised shrilly.

"I tell you it was a gorilla. I'm *sure* it was a gorilla."

"But it spoke."

"Gorillas can speak. Didn't you know that? It
didn't talk sense. It just said a gabble of words."

"It said something about garden walls and cries
for help."

"Yes, but there wasn't any *sense* in it, was there?"

"I think it was a wild man escaped from some show
or other. It looked to me just like one of those wild
men you see in shows."

"You couldn't see it. It was covered in straw."

"Yes, but I saw its eyes gleaming wildly through the straw."

"Certainly if it was human, it was mad."

William withdrew from the window.

He was still completely in the dark as to what was happening but he was dimly aware that some great ordeal lay before him.

To fortify himself against it, he put a few handfuls of chocolate biscuits into each pocket and very thoughtfully began to eat the last piece of cream-layer cake.

CHAPTER V

THE OUTLAWS AND THE PENKNIFE

GINGER was feeling aggrieved with life in general and his Aunt Amelia in particular.

Ginger's Aunt Amelia had only lately come to live in the neighbourhood. She had taken a cottage, which she shared with a literary friend, and high hopes had sprung to life in Ginger's breast at their arrival. For Aunt Amelia had not seen him since his babyhood. She was not, as were all his other aunts, conversant with his many crimes and shortcomings. She was, in Ginger's eyes, a clean slate, on which he could write a glorious tale of non-existent virtues and reap such a golden harvest as dutiful nephews may expect from high-minded, if rather short-sighted, elderly aunts.

Her first visit passed off very well. Ginger prepared himself for it with a thoroughness that left his mother speechless with surprise and bewilderment, appearing at tea with a face which he had almost flayed by relentless scrubbing, with hair plastered slickly down by a damp hair-brush, and with even his nails partially, at any rate, cleaned. He spoke and behaved with such an extremity of politeness that it was all his mother could do to conceal her anxiety. Like most mothers, she was continually urging Ginger to supreme heights of perfection, but, whenever he seemed to be approaching them, felt only anxiety for his health, and knew no real peace of mind till he had returned to his normal ways of grubbiness, unpunctuality and lawlessness.

She tried, however, to assume the expression of one whose son behaves always like a perfect little gentleman, refraining, by great effort of self-control, from asking him if he felt quite well, and conquering a strong desire to take his temperature. As far as Aunt Amelia was concerned the afternoon was a great success. She was impressed, if somewhat embarrassed, by Ginger's attentiveness. He hovered over her continually, flourishing a cake-stand and waiting patiently for her to finish what was on her plate. He said "Yes, Aunt Amelia," and "No, Aunt Amelia" in a voice of dulcet winsomeness that his own friends would not have recognised. Moreover, he had the good sense to disappear directly tea was over, well aware that a little of a good thing goes a long way and that a character of perfection is a difficult one to sustain for any length of time.

He was rewarded for the strain that he had undergone by a half-crown that Aunt Amelia pressed into his hand as he said good-bye and by overhearing her say as he closed the door: "What a well-behaved boy!"

So far so good, of course. The half-crown was received by the Outlaws (who always shared tips) with acclamation. But it was soon spent, and Ginger realised that if he meant that source of income to continue indefinitely he must get to work again and go very carefully. The other Outlaws suggested that they, too, should be introduced to Aunt Amelia in order to deepen the impression made by Ginger, but he firmly opposed this suggestion.

"No," he said, "it's jolly hard to carry on like what I did when she came to tea. You couldn't do it. I couldn't do it either if any of you were there. No, you'd better leave it to me."

"All right," said William, 'but get on with it. We've spent that half-crown, an' it's about time you were gettin' another out of her. I bet I could do it all right. I can make myself look a good deal cleaner than what you can, 'cause I've not got so many freckles——"

"You *have*," put in Ginger indignantly.

"I haven't. We counted once and I've got twenty less. Anyway, I can make myself look cleaner, 'cause I've got some white paint, an' I can paint over the dirty places on my collar, an' my ears don't stick out so much as what yours do, so it doesn't show so much when they aren't clean."

"Oh, don't they?" said Ginger, stung by this insult. "Well, let me tell you they stick out a jolly sight more."

An attempt to settle this question by physical combat left it still undecided, but the Outlaws, tiring of the subject of Ginger's aunt, turned their attention to the more congenial one of a rat hunt in a neighbouring farm.

But Ginger was aware that it was now time that he once more took up the ticklish task of playing the Perfect Boy to Aunt Amelia. As the Outlaws said, her half-crown was now a memory only and another would be welcome . . .

The next afternoon he spent half an hour on his personal appearance, wrestling long and hard with a species of indelible mud that seemed to have left its permanent mark on his brow and down one cheek. He then changed his collar, inked that portion of one leg that showed through a hole in his navy blue stocking, got a clean handkerchief, but considerably dimmed its glory but dusting his knees with it, rubbed each shoe hard upon the other stocking, leaving thick grey marks, and finally, completely satisfied with his appearance, set off in the direction of Aunt Amelia's cottage. The way was short and easy, but to Ginger it was as steep and arduous as the proverbial path of virtue, presenting at every step temptations to besmirch his comparatively immaculate appearance by burrowing in ditches, exploring tracks through the undergrowth, and climbing trees. He resisted all these temptations, and walked mincingly along, concentrating his attention on practising what he termed his "polite voice"—say "Yes, Aunt Amelia," "No, Aunt Amelia," and finally, with a shattering smirk. "Oh, *thank* you, Aunt Amelia. How kind of you!" as with outstretched and (despite vigorous applications of pumice-stone) still very grubby palm he received an imaginary half-crown.

He found Aunt Amelia working in her garden, while, seated at an open window overlooking the tiny lawn, the literary friend sat engaged in literary work. Ginger had never met the literary friend, only seen her in the distance like this, intent upon her work, occasionally raising her eyes soulfully to the tree-tops for inspiration. The literary friend wrote stories about an imaginary little boy called Michael—stories that were very much admired by elderly maiden ladies—but disliked children in real life.

"No, dear," she had said to Ginger's aunt, "don't introduce him to me. I find that real children absolutely *kill* my inspiration. There's no—no spiritual *fragrance* about them. I find that *nothing* kills my inspiration as much as a real child. I draw my inspiration from Nature alone."

"But he's a very well-behaved child," Aunt Amelia had said.

"I can't help it, dear," replied the literary friend simply. "I feel absolutely certain that there's no spiritual fragrance about him."

Ginger's aunt had to admit that perhaps there wasn't.

"But he's the politest and best-behaved child I have ever come across," she repeated.

As Ginger entered the garden, the literary friend slightly shifted her position so that she need not look at him. Certainly, despite his careful grooming, not even his best friend could have said that he suggested spiritual fragrance.

Aunt Amelia greeted him kindly, but abstractedly. It was evident that her whole attention was concentrated upon her gardening operations. With a small knife she was severing shoots from the base of the rose bushes.

"They're briar shoots, dear boy," she explained. "If allowed to grow, they would take all the goodness from the rose bush and finally kill it. It's one of those little things that a gardener can't afford to neglect.

And it's a parable—isn't it, dear boy? These little briar shoots are like the little faults that, if we allowed them to grow, would finally take all the goodness from our characters . . ."

Ginger steeled himself to endure a spate of moralising, sustaining an expression faithfully copied from William and of which William was very proud. It was an expression that was intended to convey radiant virtue and high endeavour, but that actually suggested acute dyspepsia. He consoled himself for the effort involved in keeping up this expression by fixing his thoughts on the hoped-for half-crown and its many possibilities.

"Such little faults as idleness," said Aunt Amelia.

"An' we'll jolly well get a new ball," thought Ginger, "one of those little ones that we can play with in ole Fuss-pot's history lessons."

"And greed," said Aunt Amelia.

"And some cream buns and liquorice all-sorts," thought Ginger.

"While courtesy and consideration for others," said Aunt Amelia, "are like the healthy rose shoots that will flourish and grow stronger and stronger if we keep the briar shoots well cut away."

"An' we'll get some squibs an' throw 'em down at people after dark," thought Ginger.

"And so, dear boy, we must cut away our briar shoots and strive ever upwards, and soon we will find our rose bushes strong and healthy and shining through the darkness around us, an example to others far and wide."

D

With this final flourish of mixed metaphors Aunt Amelia loked at her watch and took up her gardening basket with an air of finality.

"Did you come for anything special, dear boy?" she said.

"Yes," said Ginger absently, thinking of the half-crown, then added hastily: "No, I mean no. I mean"—intensifying the dyspeptic leer—"I mean I jus' came to see you."

"Very sweet of you, dear boy," said Aunt Amelia vaguely, "but I have to go in and write some letters now, so I'll say good-bye. I can't ask you to come in, because my friend must have absolute quiet for her work. Good-bye, dear boy."

With that she went into the cottage, leaving Ginger gazing at the closed door, the dyspeptic leer frozen upon his face. Crestfallen, he turned and walked back to the village, where William and Henry and Douglas were waiting for him.

"Well?" said William. "How much did she give you?"

"Nothin'," said Ginger morosely. "I spent hours gettin' clean an' tidy—my face still aches with washin'—an' she's not given me a ha'penny."

They looked at him sternly.

Despite his dejection he had on his homeward way deliberately succumbed to all the temptations, ditch-burrowing, tree-climbing and undergrowth-exploring, that he had resisted on his way to the cottage, and the process had completely obliterated the never-very-striking effect of cleanliness that he had attained with such labour.

"Well, of course, if you went lookin' like *that*——"
said William succinctly.

"I didn't go like this," said Ginger indignantly. "I
went lookin' cleaner than you've ever looked in your
life, only I wasn't goin' to bother to keep all that
cleanness on when she wouldn't even give me half a
crown for it, so I got it wore off on the way home."

"Well, did you *do* anything for her?" said William.

"No, there wasn't anything to do . . ."

"I spent hours gettin' clean an' tidy," said Ginger,
"an' she's not given me a ha'penny."

99

"That doesn't matter," said William sternly. "You ought to have *done* something for her. They always feel more like givin' you money if you've *done* something for them. You ought to have chopped up wood or weeded a bed or something."

"Yes, like what you did for your aunt," said Ginger indignantly, "an' pulled up all the plants she'd jus' put in an' chopped up some wood she'd jus' bought to do poker work on an' got into a jolly row. Likely she'd have given me half a crown then, isn't it?"

William, faced with these undeniable truths, became evasive.

"Oh, well, I can't stay here all day arguin' with you. Let's go an' do somethin' a bit more interestin'. We don't want her rotten old half-crown, anyway."

So the Outlaws went and did something more interesting, and completely forgot Ginger's aunt and her non-forthcomingness in the matter of half-crowns. All except Ginger. A sense of failure nagged at Ginger's heart, an overmastering desire to return to the fray and prove himself victor. When he could hold out against this desire no longer, he cleaned himself up again secretly, and set off to Aunt Amelia's cottage. He found it deserted, Aunt Amelia evidently having accompanied the literary friend on one of those Nature-communing expeditions that were necessary for the refreshment of her muse. Nothing daunted, Ginger looked about him. Though William himself had certainly had no striking success in his attempts to gain tips by gardening and wood-cutting, there had been sound sense in his advice. Surely Aunt Amelia, confronted on her return by some definite service performed for her in her absence by Ginger, would hardly have the nerve to withhold an honorarium. He looked around the neat little garden, and remembered suddenly the task upon which Aunt Amelia had been engaged on his last visit. He examined the rose trees. Now Ginger was not interested in gardening. He did not go in for fine and subtle distinctions. Briar shoots and shoots of the true rose were all the same to him. So intent had he been on the imaginary expenditure of the hoped-for half-crown that he had not listened to a word of the eloquent dissertation that Aunt Amelia had made on his last visit. He remembered the one fact that she had been cutting off shoots from the base of the rose bushes. Therefore, deduced Ginger, shoots ought to be cut off from the base of the rose bushes, and she would be grateful to him for doing it. An inspection of the rose bushes showed them to be in a terrible state of neglect. From the base of each sprang stout and healthy shoots. Ginger's spirits rose at thus finding a useful job ready to hand, a job that, he thought hopefully, should be worth at least half a crown to Aunt Amelia.

It was fortunate that it was his week for the Knife. The Knife was a magnificent affair with four blades, a corkscrew, a file, and a thing for getting stones out of a horse's hoof. William and Ginger shared it, having put together their pocket-money for several weeks in order to buy it. It was their most treasured possession, and they had it for a week each in turn. Though this arrangement led to a certain amount of recrimination, each one zealously examining the instrument after its week's absence and blaming his co-owner for any marks of wear that it might have acquired in the interval, the arrangement on the whole worked out quite satisfactorily. This week it happened to be Ginger's week. Proudly he took out the treasure, opened the largest blade, and set to work upon the rose shoots.

"You shall never have your knife back," said Aunt Amelia, "you wicked, wicked boy!"

He worked with commendable industry and thoroughness, and the little heap of rose shoots in the middle of the lawn grew to a fair-sized stack. It was while he was at work upon the last bush that Aunt Amelia returned. She stood for a moment transfixed with horror, gazing at the scene of desolation, then with a cry of rage and anguish flung herself upon the astonished Ginger, snatching the knife from his hand.

"You *wretch*," she screamed, "you've *ruined* my rose trees—*ruined* them! You hateful, *hateful* little wretch!"

She shook Ginger till his teeth chattered, then pushed him from her with a gesture of abhorrence and bent over the heap of rose shoots in an attitude of abandoned despair.

Ginger, who thought that she had suddenly gone mad and was feeling thankful to be escaping with his life, had picked himself up and reached the gate when suddenly he remembered the Knife. Aunt Amelia's frenzy had inspired him with such terror that as far as concerned himself, he would actually have forgone his beloved possession, but there was William to think of. William's week for the Knife began that very evening, and greater even than his terror of Aunt Amelia despoiled of her rose shoots was his terror of William despoiled of his knife.

His collar burst open by the violence of his shaking, his tie under one ear, his hair standing straight on end and his eyes carefully measuring the distance to the open gate, he approached Aunt Amelia, who was still bending over the stack of rose shoots in an attitude suggestive of Rachel mourning for her children.

"Please," said Ginger hoarsely, "can I have my knife back?"

Aunt Amelia swung round on him.

"No, you mayn't," she said hysterically. "*Never*. You shall *never* have your knife back. You wicked, wicked, *wicked* boy!"

Fearing another attack, Ginger took to his heels and ran all the way to the village, without stopping for breath or looking back once.

The interview with William was a heated one. Ginger took the line of self-defence. "Well, I was doin' jus' what she was doin'. *'Xactly* what she was doin'. Well, you can't blame me for her suddenly goin' mad, can you? I 'spect she'll be in an asylum to-morrow. She as near killed me as I've ever been. My head as near as possible came right off. You ought to be glad that I've escaped out of the jaws of death 'stead of makin' all this fuss over the knife."

"Well, I'm not," said William. "You could have stayed in the jaws of death for all I care, an' jolly well serve you right. I don't care if your head had come off. It doesn't seem much good on—lettin' her keep a knife like that, we're never likely to have another as good as long as we live."

"I didn't let her keep it. She snatched it off me, ravin' an' carryin' on like a mad woman, though all I'd done was *'xactly* what she was doin' herself when I went there before. I keep tellin' you I can't help people goin' mad. If you know how to stop people goin' mad p'raps you'll kin'ly tell me. Anyway it was all your fault tellin' me to go round an' do somethin' for her. Well, I went round an' did somethin' an' this is what happens."

"Oh, it's all my fault, is it?" said William. "You go an' lose that knife jus' when my week for its comin' round an' you say it's my fault."

The short, sharp struggle that followed considerably relieved their feelings, and they sat down by the roadside to discuss the question amicably.

"We've gotter get it back," said William firmly. "We can't go on letting her keep a knife like that. I shun't be surprised if it was all jus' a trick to get that knife. She knew we'd got that knife an' she cut those branches off with you there jus' to make you think she wanted it done an' bring the knife to do it, and then when you did she sprang out at you an' got the knife. I shun't be a bit surprised if it was that that happened."

This sinister aspect of the affair greatly appealed to Ginger.

"I think so, too," he said. "Why should she cut off branches herself an' then go on at me for cuttin' them off, if it wasn't? At first I thought she'd jus' gone mad, but now I think it was jus' a way of gettin' the knife."

"It was jolly clever," conceded William grudgingly, "but we're goin' to be a jolly sight cleverer gettin' it back. Let's think out a way."

"It's no good me goin' to her," said Ginger hastily, "she'll only go ravin' mad again if she sees me, an' start shakin' my head off again. It's not myself I'm thinkin' of," he added, "it's her. I don't want her to get hung for murder same as she would if she killed

105

me. I'm not frightened of her. It's only I don't want her to get hung for murder."

"Well, anyway it's not much good you goin'," agreed William, resisting the temptation to take up the challenge. "She knows you, an' she's mad at you, an' she wouldn't give you back the knife whatever you did. No, I'd better go. She's never seen me. I'll wait till to-morrow mornin'. She may've begun to feel sorry in the night. Sometimes people do. She may've jus' been in a rage an' want to make up for it. I'll plead an' reason with her, an' give her a chance to be decent, an' then if she won't be we'll have to think out a plan."

So the next morning William set off alone to Aunt Amelia's cottage. There was no one in the garden, and, with trepidation at his heart, William walked up the path and knocked at the cottage door.

A woman with short straight grey hair, wearing hornrimmed spectacles and a soulful expression opened it. Now William had not see Ginger's aunt, and it never occurred to him that this was not she. He could not know, of course, that Ginger's aunt had gone out to do some shopping, and that this was the literary friend. Nor could he know that the literary friend was expecting a child interviewer—the son of an enterprising woman editor who was featuring a series of interviews of famous writers of children's books by children, or, to be precise, by her own child. The child was a high-brow boy of eleven whose efforts, especially after the maternal touchings up, read extremely well.

William, his mind and body poised for instant flight, was unprepared for the beaming smile of welcome with which he was greeted.

"Come in, dear boy," said the literary friend.
"How splendid of you to get here so early!"

"Come in, dear boy," said the literary friend, throwing the door wide and holding out both hands to clasp his. "This is a treat, indeed! How splendid of you to get here so early! Come into my little sanctum. I allow very few people in my little sanctum, but you, of course, will be an honoured guest."

The bewildered William followed her into the sanctum. Her conscience must have been troubling her in the night. Or else Ginger had utterly misjudged her. Or else she was mad as Ginger had suggested, and with the cunning of the insane she was luring him into her parlour in order to be able to shake his head off in comfort. He sat down guardedly upon the edge of a chair and stared at her blankly.

"Now, dear," said the literary friend brightly, "before we talk about what you've come here to talk about, let's get to know each other. I want you to call me Flavia. That's the name all my writing friends call me by, and you're one of my writing friends, you know. I think you write so well, dear boy. I did so much enjoy that last thing of yours."

William was touched and gratified. He was aware that Ginger possessed a copy of his story "Dick of the Bloody Hand," but he did not know that he had shown it to his aunt. The fact that she had evidently been able to read it was an additional source of gratification to him, for it had been copied out hastily by William himself and was considered by most people—unjustly, as William thought—to be utterly illegible.

He smiled self-consciously.

"Oh, well," he said, "I'm glad you liked it."

"Of *course*, I liked it, dear boy," gushed Flavia.

"Now I do so want to get to know you, dear boy; really to *know* you."

The literary friend was determined to make a conquest of the youthful interviewer. She was hoping great things from the interview, and she knew that a lot depended on what impression she made on the boy who was to write it.

"Now, dear boy, tell me some of the fancies and imaginings that go on in your clever little head."

William gaped at her.

"The what?" he said.

"The things you pretend to yourself, dear boy. Ah, I'm sure that you live in a world of make-believe."

"Oh, yes," said William. "Yes, I do often pretend things. I often pretend I'm a cannibal cookin' people, or a pirate makin' people walk the plank, or a pre-historic monster crunchin' human bones."

Flavia winced and paled.

"Y-yes," she said. "Well, now, suppose that we talk of what you've come here to talk to me about."

"Yes," said William eagerly. He felt much encouraged by the tone of the interview, but he was aware that even so he must go carefully. He decided to lead up to the subject of the knife slowly and gradually.

"You like my little boykins?" went on Flavia coyly.

William thought this an odd way of referring to Ginger, but there was no doubt at all that Ginger's aunt was a very odd person.

"Oh, yes," he said, "I'm his greatest friend."

"How *sweet* of you to say that!" purred Flavia.

"Yes," said William, "an' he *means* to help. He really does mean to help."

"But he *does* help, dear boy," said Flavia reproachfully. "He brings sunshine and happiness into the lives of everyone around him."

William's bewilderment increased. Never had an interview run on more unexpected lines.

"Y-yes," said William. "Yes, I think that he does, too. He doesn't know much about gard'nin' p'raps, an' p'raps he makes some mistakes——"

"But he *does* know about gardening," said Flavia rather indignantly; "he's *devoted* to gardening. And he *doesn't* make mistakes . . . He's got one of those sweet child souls that are born with a sort of *understanding* of Nature."

William blinked helplessly, then made another gallant effort. "He understands other flowers, of course," he said, "but he doesn't understand *roses* very well. He doesn't know when to chop 'em off, but he wants to learn. He——"

"*Roses!*" ejaculated Flavia. "But, my dear boy, *surely* you remember the rose garden he made and tended with his own hands for the bedridden old lady—made it where she could see it from her bed—and came to look after it and cuts its blooms for her every afternoon. She liked a particular coppercoloured rose, you remember, and he took a lot of trouble growing it for her."

William struggled against an overmastering feeling of unreality.

"Not Ginger," he said weakly.

"I didn't say ginger," snapped Flavia, losing her

110

poise for a moment; "there isn't such a thing as a ginger rose. I said copper-coloured."

William tried unavailingly to reconcile this anecdote with what he knew of the history and character of Ginger.

"I don't remember jus' that," he said at last. "I remember once we found a dead cat an' we stuck it up in old General Moult's rose bed to make him come runnin' down to scare it off, an' he did an'——"

Flavia had risen with an abrupt movement. She had herself well under control, however. She remembered that in the hands of this coarse and objectionable boy lay her reputation as far as the interview was concerned. She had taken a paper from a drawer and was thrusting it into his hands.

"I think that if you will incorporate this in the article, dear boy," she said, fixing a glassy smile on him, "I needn't detain you any longer. It's a short summary of my aims and ideals. And I had a little present for you." She stopped and considered. It would never do to give this boy the present that she had purchased for the interviewer—a charming little picture called Flower Fairies. For a second she stood frowning uncertainly. She wanted to give the boy some present that would appeal to him and make him feel inclined to extol her in his account of the interview. However uncouth he seemed, he had written some quite good articles on the writers of children's books and his praise was worth something. Suddenly her face cleared, and she went from the room, returning in a few minutes with something in her hand that made William's eyes gleam.

"Take this, dear boy," she said. "It belonged to a tiresome, destructive child who maimed some of the beautiful things of Nature with it. I'm sure you'll make better use of it."

Speechless with amazement, bewilderment, and joy, William snatched the knife and, murmuring incoherent thanks, departed with it abruptly, running as fast as he could to the old barn where Ginger awaited him.

"Well?" said Ginger eagerly.

"Got it," said William breathlessly, brandishing his booty.

"How did you get it? Did you plead with her?" said Ginger.

William stood, his mind going silently back over the curious interview that had culminated in the recovery of the knife.

"She *is* mad," he said at last solemnly; "she didn't say one single word of sense all the time we were talkin'. She said you'd made a rose out of copper for an old woman."

"Me?" said Ginger.

"Yes. She was ravin' like that all the time. An' she gave me these papers . . ."

William took the sheaf of neatly written paper from his pocket and together he and Ginger studied it. It contained such words as "atmosphere", "execution," and "technique", used in wholly unintelligible connections.

"Mad!" said William again in an awestruck voice. *"Course* she's mad. This proves it. She had a mad look in her eye, too. Talkin' about people makin' roses out of coppers. An' all these pages an' pages of ravin'."

112

"Anyway, we've got the knife back," said Ginger.

"Yes, an' I'm lucky to get out without her murderin' me. There she was ravin' away as mad as mad, an' then she went and got the knife. I bet you anythin' she got it to murder me with, but I was too quick for her." A far-away look came into William's eyes as he readjusted his memories till he distinctly recalled a blood-curdling struggle with the mad woman for the possession of the knife. "Yes, I was jus' too quick for her, snatchin' it from her hand jus' before she plunged it into me. I ought to have it for a fortnight for that."

"All right, you can," said Ginger. "I feel I've had enough of it to last me more than a fortnight."

He had taken up the carefully written script and was studying it again.

"Fancy her writin' all this stuff, wastin' good paper!"

"We won't waste it," said William. "Let's make it into paper boats, an' have a race on the stream with them."

* * * * *

Ginger's aunt had returned from her shopping expedition. She laid her parcels on the hat-stand and peeped into the literary friend's sanctum.

"I suppose he's not been yet, dear, has he?" she said eagerly.

The literary friend was sitting at her desk, her head on her hands. She raised a haggard face.

"Yes, dear, he's been," she said brokenly. "He's been, and never have I ever seen a child so utterly,

utterly devoid of spiritual fragrance. He hadn't the most elementary appreciation of art. He hadn't the faintest conception of the meaning of the word literature. The delicacy, the *atmosphere* of my work meant nothing to him. I've given him my notes for the interview, but they'll convey nothing to him. *Nothing.*"

Aunt Amelia's eyes were fixed upon the garden gate.

"Who's that?" she said.

A boy was coming in at the garden gate. He carried an attaché case and wore gloves and spectacles. He looked pale and æsthetic and intellectual. He exuded spiritual fragrance from every pore. Behind him, beaming maternal pride, came a woman whom Flavia recognised as the editress of the journal.

Aunt Amelia and the literary friend stared at them in helpless bewilderment . . .

CHAPTER VI

WILLIAM AND THE WATCH AND CHAIN

WILLIAM and Robert were at present on fairly friendly terms. William found this state of things rather dull on the whole, despite his mother's frequent discourses on the Happiness of Living Together in Unity. He was, however, taking a good deal of trouble to preserve the peace, not from any love of peace for its own sake—he found a state of feud far more stimulating and exciting—but because Christmas was only a week ahead and he had learnt to tread very warily in the vicinity of the festival. Experience had taught him that the monetary value of people's presents to you depends very much on the relations that happen to exist between you and them at the time. On one occasion Robert had given him no present at all because he had taken his, Robert's bicycle to pieces to see how it was made, and, putting it together again, had omitted a vital part.

He had learnt, too, that the general state of the giver's affairs—quite apart from their pecuniary aspect—has a great effect upon the value of the gift. One whose affairs are running smoothly is more inclined to be generous than one whose affairs are awry. Therefore, he was watching Robert's affairs carefully. For Robert's Christmas present to him this year was very important. Their father was giving Robert a new watch, and Robert had hinted that he might give William his old watch for a Christmas present.

Though time mattered little enough to William, he was anxious to possess a watch and chain, and Robert's was a large, important-looking watch with a thick silver chain. It was a watch and chain that would considerably increase William's prestige among his contemporaries. And so he trod warily with Robert and watched over his affairs with an anxious eye. Robert's chief affair was, needless to say, an affair of the heart, for Robert was notoriously susceptible to feminine charm. His present inamorata was a damsel with ash blonde hair and violet eyes called Honoria Mercer, whose family had recently come to live in the village. Experience had taught William that efforts to help affairs of that sort recoil very frequently upon their author's head, so he contented himself by avoiding Honoria as far as possible, but behaving with unexampled politeness whenever a meeting was inevitable. This mode of procedure was startlingly successful—so much so that Honoria one day remarked innocently to Robert: "What a nice, polite little boy your brother is."

Robert was so staggered by this remark that he remained open-mouthed and silent for several minutes, but William, hearing of it, felt that his chances of the watch and chain were perceptibly increased.

* * * * *

The usual Christmas festivities were afoot. The Browns were giving a party the day before Christmas

116

Eve, and the week after Christmas the Botts were giving a large fancy dress dance.

William's whole attention was divided between the watch and chain and the fancy dress dance. A school friend, who could not go to the dance, had lent William his costume—that of a pantomime cat. It was a gorgeous affair with a large, grinning head, whiskers, and a furry body that buttoned up the front. William had secreted the costume in his room without telling anyone what it was. To William the essence of success of an fancy dress costume lay in its secrecy. The thought of prancing about among the guests in his cat costume, playing whatever tricks he pleased, without anyone's guessing his identity, was a very enjoyable one. The whole thing would be spoilt for him if people knew who he was. Unfortunately Ethel had seen the tail hanging out of the parcel as he carried it upstairs, and so the family knew that he was to go as an animal of some sort, but more than that he would not tell them. He hoped that there would be so many other animals that his own identity would not be guessed. He kept the drawer in which he had put it locked, and assumed a cunning, sphinx-like air when any of his family asked him about it.

The question of the watch and chain, however, was the question that loomed largest on his mental horizon.

He had made up his mind to obliterate himself as far as possible on the day of his own family's party so as not to prejudice his chances of the precious gift. In any case it was Robert's and Ethel's party and sure to be dull. They were to have charades after supper— a decision that made William snort contemptuously.

117

"Why not have a real *game*," he said, "like 'Tigers and Tamers', or something excitin' like that? Just dressin' up! Huh!"

*   *   *   *   *

Honoria was the last guest to arrive, and Robert at once took her under his care with an *empressement* that William secretly found highly amusing. He controlled his mirth, however, contenting himself with a mental mimicry of Robert's manner that gave him much inward satisfaction. He had not looked forward to the party, but his spirits rose as he entered the dining-room at the tail of the guests. He had not been allowed to take any part in these preparations, and he was much impressed by the scale of magnificence on which they had been made. He remembered, however, that his behaviour on this occasion might vitally affect his possession or non-possession of the silver watch and so he refused food himself with stoical endurance and plied Honoria with provisions till she felt almost embarrassed by his attentions. He made up for the self-restraint this imposed by staying behind in the dining-room when everyone else had gone into the drawing-room. He even followed the feast into the kitchen and stayed there, finishing up everything within reach, till the cook drove him away.

On his return to the drawing-room he found the game of charades just beginning. One side had been chosen to act, the other side to watch. Robert and Honoria were on the watching side and promptly withdrew to the morning-room to wait till the charade was ready to begin. Robert did not believe in wasting time . . . William was on the acting-side, and he accompanied the others into the hall, beginning to feel excited despite himself. He had thoughtfully filled his pockets with chocolate biscuits and munched them busily as the others discussed what word to act.

Occasionally he made a suggestion, but as no one took any notice of it he finally gave his whole attention to the chocolate biscuits. Suddenly he discovered that Ethel was addressing him . . . Ethel, it appeared, was to represent the Queen of Sheba, and William was to be her slave.

"Go and put on my happi coat, William," she said. "It's hanging behind the door. You can hitch it up at the waist if it's too long, and you'll find a scarf in my top drawer than you can make into a turban."

William obeyed these orders zestfully. He secretly enjoyed dressing up, though he pretended to despise it. The effect of the happi coat and scarf-turban was certainly impressive. But there was something missing. He had once seen a picture of the Queen of Sheba with a page in attendance and the page had been black. His face at any rate . . . He came downstairs to the hall to consult someone, but it was empty. The actors were all changing in various bedrooms. Screams of laughter came from his mother's bedroom where Ethel and her friends were dressing . . . He wondered whether to go and ask Ethel, then decided not to in case she said it wasn't necessary. No, best confront them with a face already blackened: they couldn't very well tell him to go and take it off then. The next question was how to get the blacking. It would be useless to go to the kitchen and ask for it. The cook had already chased him out in fury. He decided to creep out into the garden by the side door, go round to the back of the house and get the blacking through the pantry window. He'd put the blacking on his face outside in the garden to prevent all possibility of anyone seeing him and telling him not to, and on the way back he'd just look in at the morning-room window to see how Robert was getting on with Honoria. It was very important to him that Robert should get on well with Honoria and so be in a good temper—and consequently generously inclined—on Christmas Day.

* * * * *

Robert was finding Honoria rather heavy going, but this did not in any way decrease his fervour. On the other hand it rather increased it, for Robert, true to his race, found difficulty a stimulant, not a deterrent. Honoria seemed bent on discussing her favourite masculine qualities, which seemed a promising enough topic in the circumstances, but, despite all Robert's efforts, she refused to pass from the general to the particular.

"What I really admire *most* in a man," said Honoria fervently, "is courage."

Robert assumed a modest air.

"I'm told," he said casually, "that I once met a bull in a field when I was little more than a child and showed no fear at all."

"I expect you thought it was a cow," said Honoria carelessly, and continued: "Courage is a quality that seems to be dying out among modern men. I mean, you've only got to read historical novels to see that.

The things they do in historical novels! Really *brave* things, I mean. Well, I don't know a single modern man who would do the things people do quite as a matter of course in historical novels. I mean, they'll fight whole crowds of people and get wounded all over and then they'll run away so fast that no one can catch them, and then they'll fight more men and escape out of prison, climbing down rocks and jumping over precipices and that sort of thing—and I've just read one where the man's attacked by a whole pack of savage bloodhounds and strangles them every one, and then climbs right up the outside of a high tower to rescue the girl who's imprisoned there . . ."

Robert cast his eyes back over the nineteen years of his life, but could think of no exploits to compete with that.

"It sounds like something on the pictures," he said coldly.

"Oh, the pictures!" she said contemptuously. "All the things you see on the pictures are faked, you know. Dummies and things. They don't thrill me in the least. No, it's real courage in real life that thrills me, and there simply doesn't seem to be any of it left . . ."

"I've got a little car, you know," said Robert, trying to change the subject; "it's just one of those baby things but I can touch sixty on her quite easily."

Honoria shook her ash blonde head sadly.

"There's no *bravery* in that," she said.

"I know," said Robert; "I never said there was. I was just telling you. I thought it possible that you'd be interested."

"No," said Honoria, "I'm not interested in cars. I don't know why. They simply don't thrill me."

"I was playing rugger the other day," said Robert modestly, "and I got two goals and a try all within half an hour. They were the only goals anyone got all through the game. There were a lot of people watching. I felt quite embarrassed when they cheered . . ."

But the violet blue eyes remained dreamy and aloof.

"Games don't thrill me either," said Honoria. "Not at all. I don't know why. It's the way I'm made, I suppose. It's *courage* that thrills me, not just *strength* . . . You know, I once heard of a man and he was alone in the house and he saw a perfectly *dreadful* face looking in at him through the window, and without a moment's hesitation he smashed the window and——"

Robert had turned instinctively to the window and there met the blackened face of William. He did not recognise William, and certainly the face as a face was terrifying enough, the whites of the eyes showing up horribly against the shining blackness. Robert sprang up with a yell of terror and plunged towards the door. Honoria, too, had turned to the window, but William had by now disappeared.

"What on earth's the matter?" said Honoria.

"A face!" gasped Robert. "There was a most *ghastly* face at the window."

Honoria gave him an icy glance from her violet blue eyes, then swept from the room without a word.

Explanations, of course, only made the situation worse. For William, standing in the full light of the hall, looked a harmless enough object, despite his blackened face.

"And anyway," said Honoria distantly, "even if there had been danger—well, to run away yourself and leave me there——!"

Words failed her . . . She gave him another douche of violet blue ice and turned away.

For the rest of the evening she ignored him completely, devoting herself to his friend and rival, Jameson Jameson, whom hitherto she had treated with indifference.

Robert managed to obtain a short interview with her before she went home . . . In it he passionately protested his courage and devotion, and offered to do any deed of daring she chose to name in order to prove his mettle, but it was useless.

"No," she said, "I'm sorry, but I'm like that I simply can't forgive cowardice."

"But you don't understand," pleaded Robert. "I'll do anything . . . *anything*. Honestly. I'm not a coward. Ask anyone who knows me . . ."

"I prefer to trust my own eyes," said Honoria icily, and left him protesting passionately to the empty air.

He lost no time in blaming William for the state of affairs, and William in his turn protested passionately, but in vain.

"How was I to *know?*" he said. "I was jus' lookin' in as I was passin'. Well, there's no lor against jus' lookin' in at a window as you're passin', is there? I didn't mean to do any harm."

"Terrifying her like that!" said Robert fiercely—for Robert, of course had not given William quite a true

123

account of the affair. "Naturally she doesn't want to have anything more to do with a man whose brother goes about playing tricks of that sort."

William, who hoped still to possess the watch and chain despite this contretemps, behaved with un-exampled meekness, but Robert's wrath did not abate. During the evening, when someone mentioned that he was to have a gold watch for his Christmas present, Mrs. Brown said:

"And you're going to give your old one to William, aren't you, dear?"

Whereupon Robert snorted sardonically and said:

"No. I should jolly well think I'm not. I'm going to sell it."

During the next day William tried hard to think of some way of overcoming Robert's anger and so obtaining the watch and chain on which his heart was set, but no plan occurred to him. Probably, of course, if he saved Robert's life Robert might melt towards him and give him the watch and chain, but short of that he could think of nothing to meet the situation.

A fair had come to the village, and the Browns had decided to pay it a visit on Christmas Eve. They all set off together, Robert and William ignoring each other completely. Robert secretly felt a little nervous. He knew that William regarded himself as unfairly treated in the matter of the watch and chain, and, though determined not to give it to him, he was pre-pared for reprisals.

William did not as a rule accept unfair treatment without retaliation, and, glancing at his freckled expressionless face, Robert suspected that even now he was evolving some plan of revenge.

On reaching the fair ground the first people they met were Jameson Jameson and Honoria. Jameson Jameson gave them a sheepish grin and Honoria pretended not to see them. Robert ground his teeth and threw a furious glance at William. William maintained his impassive demeanour and as soon as possible escaped from his family to wander round the fair ground himself and drown his troubles in Aunt Sally and Houp-la, and brandy snaps and coconuts . . . The rest of the family also wandered off, and Robert was left alone, leaning morosely against the support of a booth. He could see Jameson Jameson and Honoria . . . they had just descended from the roundabout and were standing engrossed in animated and very amicable conversation near him, but still ignoring him. Honoria's scorn of him had made her all the more desirable in his eyes, and his misery and sense of desolation were almost unbearable.

Suddenly, to his amazement, a large, shaggy head appeared round the corner of the booth, and he found himself gazing into what was apparently the face of a lion . . . The vague suspicions of William that had been smouldering in his heart all day sprang to life in a second. He remembered the fancy dress costume— "some sort of an animal"—that William had kept so secret. This, then, was the trick the kid had been planning . . . to dress up in his costume and try to expose him in public as a coward—a point on which he was just now so peculiarly sensitive.

He made a threatening gesture at the face.

"Get off with you," he said. "I know who you are and I've had enough of your tricks."

The creature receded a few steps. Robert followed it. His anger now was beyond control. He'd *show* the kid!

"Go straight home," he said, "and take that thing off, and I'll jolly well give you something to think of instead of monkey tricks like this . . ."

The creature backed before him, and Robert followed it, still with threatening words and gestures. So inflamed was he with fury that he did not see people fleeing on all sides, climbing tent-poles, barricading themselves in the caravans.

Across the open fair ground backed the lion, followed threateningly by Robert, the scene watched with breathless terror by the spectators from their hiding-places. Then suddenly Robert saw something that turned his blood to ice. He saw William watching the scene from the doorway of a tent, a piece of coconut in one hand, a brandy snap in the other, his mouth open wide with amazement. But before Robert, realising suddenly the true state of affairs, could turn to flee, two men had come up, secured the animal with ropes, and were leading it off. Turning round, dazed, and trembling, Robert saw Jameson Jameson adorning the top of the flag-pole, while Honoria stood at the bottom of it, her hands clasped, her eyes, alight with hero-worship, fixed ardently upon Robert.

The spectators rushed from their hiding-places and crowded round Robert, congratulating, praising. He had recovered himself quickly.

"Oh, that's nothing," he said lightly. "It's simply

that I never have been frightened of lions. They simply don't frighten me."

He brushed them aside and made his way to where Honoria still stood, gazing at him in ardent admiration.

"Oh, can you ever forgive me for doubting you?" she said.

"Of course, of course," said Robert generously. "Don't mention it."

"When I saw the awful creature standing there and *him*"— with a scornful glance at Jameson, who was slowly and ungracefully descending his flag-pole—"getting up that thing and not caring whether I was eaten alive or not, and *you* . . . Oh, I've never seen anything so *brave* in all my life!"

Robert straightened his tie with a modest, deprecating gesture.

"Oh, that's nothing," he said. "I'm simply not frightened of lions, that's all. As a matter of fact, I'm not frightened of anything. I was just having a little joke on you the other night, pretending to be frightened. I'd no idea you were going to take it seriously . . ."

"I can see now how stupid it was of me," she said. "You *do* forgive me, don't you?"

"Of course," said Robert.

Someone came up and reported that the keepers had said that it was very plucky of Robert to tackle the beast, as it had a very uncertain temper.

"Oh, I could see that," said Robert. "That was the first thing I noticed. I thought: 'The beast's got a very uncertain temper. I'd better get him back to his cage as quickly as possible, or he'll be doing some harm . . .' "

"Oh, how brave of you," said Honoria again, fervently. "Let's get out of the crowd; I'm sure you're tired."

"Oh, no," said Robert, "not a bit. There's nothing in what I did. I'm simply not afraid, that's all. As a matter of fact," he admitted, "I don't know the meaning of the word fear."

"I think you're *wonderful*," breathed Honoria once more.

Jameson Jameson came up to them, looking rather sheepish.

"Congratulations, Robert," he said, and to Honoria: "I say, I'm frightfully sorry. I want to explain. I——"

But it was his turn for a douche of violet-blue ice. Honoria turned on her heel and left him, drawing Robert with her.

"The *coward*!" she said between her teeth. "Oh, the *coward*!"

"You mustn't blame him too much," said Robert magnanimously. "After all, some chaps can't *help* being afraid of danger, you know."

"Oh, never mind him. Now tell me everything you thought and felt when you did it."

"Well," said Robert, "the first thing I thought of when I saw it was you. I thought: 'I must get this beast back to its cage before it attacks Honoria. I must defend her from it and if it kills me—well, it won't matter very much after all now that she doesn't believe in me any longer.' "

"Oh, *Robert*! . . . Robert, will you *ever* forgive me for doubting you? I *know* now that you're the bravest man in the world."

"Oh, well," said Robert modestly, "I shouldn't put it quite like that."

"I should," persisted Honoria. "It was—oh, it was simply *heroic*."

They were passing the open door of the tent where William stood watching them, still transfixed by amazement. Robert felt generously inclined. Moreover, he realised that indirectly he owed his good fortune to William.

He took off his watch and chain and slipped them carelessly into William's hands as he passed . . .

E

CHAPTER VII

WILLIAM AND THE FISHERMAN

EVERY June William's father went alone to a country inn for ten days' fishing. William had often begged to be allowed to accompany him, but his requests had always been met by such an uncompromising refusal that he had long since given up all hope. This year, however, to his surprise and delight Fate seemed to be on his side. He had had chicken-pox, and the doctor had decreed that a change of air was necessary before he returned to school.

His mother could not leave her housekeeping duties. The various relatives to whom (though without much real hope) she confided the problem replied kindly and sympathetically, but carefully refrained from inviting William to stay with them.

"You're going away next week, aren't you, dear?" said Mrs. Brown to her husband innocently.

He looked at her suspiciously.

"If you mean will I take William," he said firmly, "I most decidedly will not."

But he felt much less firm on the point than he sounded.

If the doctor said that William must have a change of air and he was the only member of the family going away, he didn't see how he could very well refuse to take him with him. He wrote to several relatives who had not yet been approached asking them bluntly if they would care to have William for a few days. They replied as bluntly that they would not.

"Mind you," said Mr. Brown to his wife after having received the last of these replies, "if that boy comes with me, he must look after himself. I'm not going to be responsible for him in any way."

William, on learning that he was to go with his father on the fishing holiday that had been his Mecca from babyhood, could hardly contain his excitement.

He imagined himself accompanying his father and his friends upon all their fishing expeditions. He saw himself making huge catches of trout and salmon before admiring crowds of onlookers. His father seemed to be taking innumerable fishing-rods with him, and William, ever an optimist, thought that he would probably lend him the ones he was not actually using. If his father happened to be using all his rods at once, William then would use his own fishing-rod—a home-made implement consisting of a stick, a piece of string and a bent pin, with which he had distinguished himself at minnow catching in all the local streams. If it would catch minnows, there was, William decided, no reason why it should not catch trout or even salmon . . . He set off with his father, full of hope, confidence, and excitement.

For the first day he was busy assimilating his impressions. The inn—its *clientèle* consisted entirely of angling enthusiasts—was full of large, purposeful-looking men to whom fishing was real, fishing was earnest; men who treated with silent contempt any

131

remark that did not bear directly and intelligently upon the subject of fishing. At meal-times they sat round a large table in the dining-room in a grim silence broken only by such remarks as: "There was a good hatch of May-fly about quarter-past three," or "They were rising all right, but we couldn't find out what they were taking." Directly after breakfast they would garb themselves in all-enveloping diver-like costumes, collect their tackle and set off, still silent, grim, and purposeful, each to his favourite haunt.

They would not return till the evening and then it was the custom that each should silently and with modest pride lay his catch upon the marble-slabbed hat-stand in the hall of the inn—each catch carefully separate and apart from the others. No one talked of his catch. He merely laid it upon the hat-stand and waited for someone to ask whose it was. News of each catch spread quickly through the community. After dinner again the sportsmen sallied out, solemnly, purposefully, grimly, for the "night rise".

William watched all this with breathless interest. The thought of forming a part of such a community filled him with a fierce and burning pride.

On the first day his father asked him if he would like to come out with him in a boat, and William eagerly agreed. He found the day disappointing. His father landed him on an island in the lake with an empty tobacco box and instructions to catch May-fly in the bushes. William caught three, then became bored and began to experiment with the damming of a small stream and finally to attempt the draining of a miniature bog into which he sank up to his knees.

When his father returned for him, the three May-flies had escaped and his father, who immediately on reaching the fishing community had yielded to its pervading atmosphere of grim purposefulness, was coldly reproachful. The rest of the day was merely boring. The boatman would not let William try to row. His father would not let him try to fish. He got hopelessly entangled in a spare rod; he accidentally dropped overboard a box of flies that were unobtainable locally; he was bitten in the hand by a trout that he thought was dead, and thereupon gave a yell that put every other fish for miles around upon its guard.

He disgraced himself completely and finally by standing up to stretch away an attack of pins and needles, and overbalancing upon his father's rod and breaking it.

"I know one thing," said his father feelingly, "and that is that you're jolly well not coming out with me in the boat again."

William was not in any way perturbed by the sentence. It had been a boring and unsatisfactory day and he was convinced that a day spent by himself on dry land would be a much more enjoyable affair.

To his surprise and disgust, however, his father refused to lend him one of his rods. His father, it appeared, needed all his rods—either for "dapping" or "trolling" or "casting".

William considered that these people made far too complicated an affair of the simple exercise of fishing and set off alone with his home-made rod, a packet of sandwiches, and a basket lent to him for his "catch" by the landlady.

He found a suitable stream, fixed a worm on to the bent pin at the end of his line, and began to fish. His luck was amazing. He caught minnow after minnow. He worked hard all the morning and all afternoon and returned in the evening with a laden basket. The other fishermen had not yet returned. The marble top of the hat-stand gleamed empty and inviting. William poured the contents of his basket upon it. They covered it completely with a shining heap of minnows. William gazed at them with fond pride. Then he got a piece of paper, wrote on it, "William Brown", and put it on the top of the silvery heap. That done, glowing with triumph, he awaited the return of the other fishermen. Not one of them had ever completely filled the marble slab with a single catch like this. He had no doubt at all that he would be the hero of the evening.

Soon he heard the sound of someone approaching and stepped back modestly into the shadow. One of the fishermen—a stalwart young man with a projecting jaw and hooked nose—entered. He looked at the minnow-filled slab, scowled angrily. swept the whole gleaming heap on to the floor with an outraged gesture, rang the bell, said to the housemaid: "Clear up that mess," then with slow deliberate care placed a row of twelve trout on the slab.

William was speechless with indignation at the affront. His first impulse was to hurl himself savagely upon the young man, his second, based upon a consideration of the young man's powerful and muscular frame, was to contain his fury as best he could till an opportunity for a suitable revenge offered itself.

Up to now the fishermen had been identical in

William's eyes. They were all large, single-purposed, unsmiling men dressed in enormous waders and devoid of any ideas outside the world of fishing.

Now each detached himself from the mass, as it were, and assumed distinct personalities. There appeared to be two camps of them. The elder ones forgathered in the smoking-room. William's father, who had come to the conclusion many years ago that William was quite capable of looking after himself, and who in any case had from the beginning announced his intention of not allowing him to interfere with his holiday, belonged to the elder camp, and in order to preserve the illusion of a Williamless holiday, had from the first forbidden William to enter the smoking-room. So William, perforce, spent his time with the younger fishermen, and it was therefore the younger fishermen whom he particularly studied.

The leader among them was the muscular youth addressed by his familiars as "Archie" who had swept William's magnificent catch so contemptuously on to the floor. Archie was the most skilful fisherman of the party. The others humbly asked his advice and appraised his prowess. Archie's row of trout on the hat-stand slab was always longer than that of any of the others. Archie, moreover, knew the owner of a specially prolific reach of river, and had permission to fish there. He would return from his fishing expedition in this reach laden with spoils and more blatantly pleased with himself each time.

Archie was admired, his advice was sought on all sides, but not even his dearest friends could deny that Archie was overbearing and conceited. It soon became evident that he disliked William as much as William disliked him. The episode of the minnows seemed to him to be a deliberate affront to his dignity, and the presence of William among the party a perpetual outrage. He found fault with William continually, pushing him out of his way whenever he met him, with such lack of ceremony that more than

William was speechless with indignation.

once he sent him sprawling to the ground. He made loud remarks in William's hearing on the unsuitability of having "kids mucking about the place".

"It's never happened before," he said, "and I hope to goodness that it'll never happen again. If it does I shall look out for another place."

William bided his time. He studied his enemy. There was no pretence about Archie's skill as a fisherman. William even followed him secretly down to his private post in the preserved reach and saw him catching trout after trout with an ease and ability that, despite his dislike, William could not help admiring.

He watched him standing in the swirling current in mid-stream up to his waist still fishing with ease and ability. Certainly in his capacity as fisherman Archie was invulnerable. William tried to find some capacity in which he might be vulnerable, but could find none. For Archie seemed to be nothing but a fisherman. He seemed to have no instincts and desires but those of a fisherman. He seemed to function wholly and entirely upon the fishing plane.

The days passed swiftly by, and William, still enduring Archie's ceaseless snubs, almost began to give up hope of getting his own back. The last weekend of the holiday had arrived, and still Archie had revealed no weakness through which an enemy might avenge himself. His armour seemed to be jointless. Then—two days before William and his father were to return home—there arrived at the inn an elderly fisherman with his daughter.

The elderly fisherman was negligible enough, but

the daughter was not. Even William could see at a glance that this was the sort of girl who made things hum. She had dimples, and dark, curling lashes shading eyes of the deepest blue. Her complexion was smooth and flawless. She had a shatteringly beautiful smile. And William, watching his enemy with ceaseless vigilance, realised at once that Archie was smitten, utterly and uncompromisingly smitten. Smitten, as the saying is, hip and thigh. Only the day before, Archie, after complaining for the thousandth time of having "kids messing about the place," had added: "But thank heaven, at least there aren't women this year." But now William saw his tanned and healthy countenance deepen to a rich beetroot immediately his eyes fell upon this latest arrival.

The girl, whose name was Claribel, while apparently ignoring the youthful sportsmen and devoting herself entirely to her father, was obviously fully aware of the impression she had made. For not only Archie was smitten, but all the other members of the younger camp were smitten too.

It did not take long for the first shyness to wear off and then began the competition for the damsel's notice. And here Archie's friends, who should have rallied round him, basely deserted him. They did not sing his praises. They did not boost him to the skies as the world's best fisherman. They left him to sing his own praises and boost himself to the skies. To do him justice he was not backward. He boosted himself well and good. He enumerated his recent catches. He discribed how he alone of all the fishing party could fish with ease when up to his arms in a swirling torrent.

138

"It's partly a question of balance," he said, "and partly that I'm—well, I'm a fairly good fisherman, of course."

And Archie stroked his microscopic moustache complacently.

At first Claribel was amused, but gradually she became impressed.

"Come out in the boat with me to-morrow," said Archie, "I'm sure you'll enjoy it. I mean I'm sure you'll find it quite interesting."

Claribel agreed, and William saw yet another triumph in store for the hated Archie. For Claribel, he realised at once, despite her affectation of hauteur, belonged to the class of "soppy girls". She swam with the stream and went with the crowd. If fishing were the fashion, then Claribel bags the best fisherman. And without doubt, Archie was the best fisherman. William was very thoughtful that evening.

"Who's the kid?" he heard Claribel ask of Archie.

And Archie replied contemptuously:

"A wretched little oik someone's brought with him."

The next morning was a perfect fishing morning, and Claribel, dressed very fetchingly in pale pink organdie, set off gaily to the river with Archie. He helped her into the boat with a courteous gesture, then the boatman pushed off.

"Isn't this jolly!" William heard Claribel say gaily. "Just like a picnic."

William unobtrusively followed, the progress of the boat along the bank, slipping from bush to bush. The strident voice of Archie, enumerating his fishing exploits, reached him clearly across the water.

They reached a point in the river where, only the day before, Archie had stood in mid-stream, the water up to his arm-pits, "casting" with magnificent aplomb, and catching trout after enormous trout. He lowered himself from the boat and took up his stand, a smile of proud anticipation on his lips. He took up his stand and threw his line. Claribel watched him from the boat.

"Now start catching all those fishes you talk about," she said gaily.

Archie had cast his line stylishly enough, but the complacent expression of his face was giving way to uneasiness.

He smiled a ghastly smile at her and said: "Oh, yes . . . you jolly well wait a few minutes . . ." Then the uneasiness of his expression deepened to panic.

"Hi!" he called suddenly, dropping his rod and clutching wildly at the air. "Hi! Help!"

The boatman hastily brought the boat up to him. He clutched frenziedly at the boatside and then at Claribel. He hung dripping round Claribel's neck. "I'm drowning!" he shouted. "Take me out quick!"

The boat rocked frantically. The boatman and Claribel between them dragged Archie into it. Claribel rendered this assistance involuntarily. Archie, having clasped his arms about her neck in his first spasm of terror, refused to unclasp them, and, long before his large and struggling body was safely landed in the boat, the pale pink organdie was a sodden mass, and Claribel was weeping with fury.

"I couldn't help it," panted Archie. "I t-tell you I was going under. I'd lost my balance. I'd have d-d-drowned if I hadn't caught hold of you. My waders were flooded. I can't t-t-think how. It's a miracle I wasn't drowned. I can't think *how* I wasn't drowned."

"I wish you had been," burst out Claribel passionately. "You've ruined my dress."

"Here's the hole, sir," said the boatman, pointing to an almost imperceptible slit just above the waist of Archie's waders.

"I can't think how it came there," said Archie. "They were all right yesterday." Then to Claribel: "I couldn't help it, I tell you."

"Of *course* you could help it," stormed Claribel. "Making a fool of yourself and me like that! *Deliberately* ruining everything I've got on. I'm soaked, and my dress is *ruined*, I tell you. Take me home at once. I shall never speak to you again as long as I live."

The boatman retrieved the rod, and rowed them back to the landing-place, Archie protesting loudly, Claribel, who had had her say, now gazing over his head with an expression of icy contempt.

William did not come out of cover till they had vanished from view. Then he walked slowly homeward, tenderly fingering the penknife that had punctured Archie's waders and self-esteem.

But William never left anything to chance. He himself had an elder sister of great personal charm, and he had long studied with interest and perpetual surprise the way of a maid with a man. He had learnt that the more angry and unrelenting the maid seems at the actual moment of provocation, the sooner is she likely to relent. So that when he reached the inn he was not surprised to find Claribel and Archie on friendly terms again. Claribel had changed into a blue linen dress that was very becoming, so becoming in fact that she could not help feeling on good terms with herself and the whole world. She was even viewing the episode through a haze of glamour and looking on herself as having rescued Archie from a watery grave. Archie, with more sense than William would have given him credit for, was encouraging this view.

"I simply don't know what I'd have done if you hadn't happened to be there," he was saying.

"Well, of course," said Claribel modestly, "I always have been considered rather fearless. I mean, I do know how to keep my head in a crisis. I just saw what to do and did it. I'm like that."

"It was wonderful of you," said Archie fervently, "simply *wonderful*. I believe that it's the first morning I've ever come in without catching a single fish. I'll go down to the river this afternoon, however, and see if I can make up for it."

"I expect you will if all I hear of your fishing is true," said Claribel sweetly.

It was very trying for William after all the trouble he had taken to see Archie resuming his old intolerable conceit and Claribel gradually softening towards him. But he had prepared for this, too. Not for nothing had he trudged yesterday into the nearest market town. Moreover, his knowledge of human nature served him well. He was sure that Claribel, after her morning's wetting, would not want to accompany Archie on his afternoon's fishing expedition.

So Archie set off alone. He was away for several hours, and when he returned he proudly laid twelve trout upon the hat-stand, and went to summon Claribel to admire.

He did not see William slip into the hall as he went out of it. When he returned to it with Claribel he saw no difference in the fish that he had laid there. It was Claribel who discovered a wet and illegible fishmonger's ticket adhering to one of them, Claribel whose small but perfect nose discovered the distinctly unpleasant odour of the thirteenth fish—unlucky enough for Archie—that William had deftly introduced into the row. It was in vain that Archie protested and pleaded, in vain that he brought proof incontrovertible that he had actually caught the fish.

Claribel's anger of the afternoon had returned redoubled.

"A nasty, mean, low-down trick to play on me!" she fumed. "A cheat, that's what you are! A nasty, common cheat! Trying to make me think you'd caught them when you'd bought every *one* of them at a fishmonger's—and one of them bad at that! First you try to drown me—yes, and nearly *did* drown me. I could get you put in prison for attempted murder for this morning. I'm sure I could. It was a plot to *murder* me. I don't believe there was a hole in your waders. Or if there was you put it there. And then when you've not been able to murder me you try to make a fool of me by pretending to have caught fish when you've been out to buy them. I hate you, and

I'll never speak to you again as long as I live. I always thought fishermen were cheats and liars, and now I know they are. *And* murderers. I hate all of you. I shan't stay a minute longer in the beastly place."

Leaving Archie opening and shutting his mouth silently like one of his own expiring fish, she swept into the smoking-room, where her father sat swopping fishing yarns with some members of the elder camp. He was surprised but in no way discomposed by his daughter's sudden decision to go home. He had long ago accustomed himself to sudden changes of plans on the part of his female belongings. Moreover, he knew that she had only accompanied him on an impulse, leaving behind her several interesting "affairs" from which a good deal of kick could still be extracted. He had had a suspicion that the place would fail to supply the excitement that was necessary to a girl of Claribel's temperament, and on the whole was not sorry to hear her decision.

"All right, my dear," he said mildly, "but I'm afraid you can't leave this minute, because there isn't a train till to-morrow afternoon."

She did not come downstairs that evening. She spent it packing in her bedroom, while Archie hung about the hall, still opening and shutting his mouth silently, as if practising passionate speeches of protestation.

The next morning after breakfast Claribel directed the shattering smile at William and said: "Will you come for a walk with me this morning, William?"

William accepted the invitation with apparent

eagerness, though he remained completely unshattered by the smile. He knew that Claribel had fixed on the "wretched little oik" with a true womanly intuition of what would be most galling to Archie. They spent the whole morning together. William found it intolerably boring. Claribel was the most limited human being whom he had ever met. She was wholly ignorant on the subject of pirates or smugglers or Red Indians. She was not interested in climbing trees, or damming streams, or getting through barbed-wire fences, or exploring the countryside. She was frightened of spiders, and she did not know a toad from a frog. Relations became definitely strained between them as the morning wore on, and Claribel grew more and more irritable, especially when William took her a short cut back to the inn that led directly through a bog. William persisted that the bog was now all right, as he had drained it three days before, but Claribel's dainty shoes bore ample evidence that this statement of William's erred on the side of optimism. Her resentment against the wretched Archie, however, still blazed so brightly that as soon as they came within sight of the inn she turned her shattering smile on to William again and began to talk to him with every appearance of affectionate interest.

The sight of Archie lurking morosely in the hall when they entered assured her that her efforts were not being wasted.

During lunch she continued to talk brightly to William. After lunch the station bus drew up at the front door, and Claribel, attired for the journey, stepped into it. Archie sprang forward desperately.

"Listen!" he said. "Just listen! Just let me explain!"

But Claribel turned to William with the shattering smile and said:

"Good-bye, William darling, and thank you so much for being so sweet to me."

Then the bus swept her away, still waving effusively to William. Archie gave a hollow laugh, and William slipped away before Archie should try to find outlet for his feelings.

William and his father were going home the next day, so it was not difficult for William to avoid Archie's vengeance in the interval.

Failing to find William, Archie wreaked his vengeance on the fishes and brought in a phenomenal catch that he flung carelessly upon the slab, repeating the hollow laugh.

"Did you enjoy it, William dear?" asked William's mother when he reached home.

William considered the question in silence for a moment, then said:

"Yes, on the whole, I did—quite . . . especially the end part."

CHAPTER VIII

WILLIAM AND THE DRUG TRAFFICKER

ROBERT was, of course, indirectly responsible for the whole thing. William had been kept indoors with a cold for a week, and Robert had good-naturedly lent him a few of the volumes with which he beguiled his less highbrow moments. Most of them dealt with murderers and amateur detectives who were now almost as familiar to William as his own beloved pirates and Red Indians. But one of them opened up entirely new ground. It was concerned with the drug traffic, and in the book the traffic was carried on by people of apparently the highest respectability. Elderly maiden ladies of impeccable appearance handed small twists of paper to simple old men whose interests seemed to centre entirely in their gardens. Clergymen with long, white beards threw minute packages from carriage windows as trains flashed by stations, and these were picked up as if quite casually by earnest-looking men wearing the Salvation Army uniform.

The seeming respectability—even holiness—of every member of the gang made the work of the hero, who was engaged in tracking them, extremely difficult.

William found the book so engrossing that he read it far into the night, propping up a rug against his bedroom door so that his mother would not see the line of light beneath it when she came to bed. The next morning he looked on the world around him with changed eyes. So powerful an impression had the book made on him that even the sight of his mother handing a ten-shilling note to the baker's man roused in his feelings of the deepest suspicion. He began to haunt the Vicar, the doctor, the superintendent of the Sunday School, and the many elderly ladies of impeccable appearance who lived in the neighbourhood. His hopes at first were very high, but as the days passed and he failed to find any actual proof of guilt, he grew tired of shadowing them, and would have forgotten the affair entirely had it not been for the arrival of a college friend of Robert's who had been invited to spend part of the vacation at the Browns'. He was nineteen, the same age as Robert, and of such a particularly guileless appearance—mild blue eyes, lank hair, and a high-pitched voice—that William's interest and suspicions sprang at once to life again. The guest was, moreover, of a studious turn of mind, and insisted on Robert's reading with him for an imminent exam during the greater part of the morning.

William was convinced that this wholly unnatural display of zeal marked some nefarious plot. He shadowed him continually, carefully examining the soles of his shoes, the back of his clothes-brush, his mattress, and various other places suitable for the concealment of drugs. The friend—his name, Rupert Bergson, was in itself almost a proof of guilt—obeyed the convention by which small brothers of eleven are as completely ignored as if they did not exist, and, following Robert's example, never acknowledged William's presence by word or look. This attitude was to William a further proof—if further proof were needed —that Rupert Bergson was engaged in some criminal pursuit. His ignoring of William proved a guilty conscience. He was afraid of giving himself away.

One morning Rupert set off for a walk alone, leaving Robert reading in his bedroom. William shadowed him with his usual elaborate air of secrecy, his coat collar turned up, his cap well over his eyes.

Instead of going for one of the walks that he and Robert usually took, Rupert followed the short cut to the station through the fields and churchyard. William enjoyed shadowing him through the churchyard, dodging from tombstone to tombstone. It was a proceeding that appealed strongly to his sense of the dramatic. When the guest reached the station William at first thought that he had realised his suspicions and had decided on flight.

Crouching behind the only luggage truck William eagerly awaited events. Rupert Bergson stood upon the platform his hands in his pockets unaware of the stern gaze that William bent on him from behind his luggage truck. Suddenly a train came through the station. It did not stop, but as it passed a youth who was leaning out of a carriage window threw a piece of paper folded into the shape of a cocked hat at Rupert's feet. Rupert picked it up, put it in his pocket, then set off briskly homewards. So impressed was William by this confirmation of his darkest suspicions that he remained absent-mindedly crouching behind his truck till the porter—an old enemy—rudely interrupted his reveries, seized him by the collar and ejected him urgently from the premises.

William picked himself up, gave a short, harsh laugh, which was meant to express dark hints of vengeance on the porter, then ran off quickly after his quarry, catching him up just as he reached the Browns' house. He followed him into the hall and up the stairs. Rupert opened the door of Robert's bedroom and entered. Before the door was shut William heard Robert say: "Got it?" and heard Rupert's reply: "Yes . . . he threw it out from the train."

William went slowly and thoughtfully downstairs. So Robert was in it, too. That rather complicated matters. He could not simply inform the police of the matter if Robert was in it, too. He could not very well hand over his only brother to certain penal servitude . . . He must go very carefully. The situation called for finesse and resource.

All that afternoon the two remained in Robert's bedroom with the door shut, and William, hovering about outside, imagined them lying on luxurious divans (Robert's room did not contain any luxurious divans, but in his book drug takers and luxurious divans were so intrexicably connected that William could not imagine one without the other) smoking pipes of opium and inhaling cocaine. They emerged at tea-time looking tired and wan, and William shook his head sorrowfully over their plight. He decided to appeal to Robert's better self and, approaching him when he was alone in the morning-room, said earnestly:

"Robert, I'd give it up if I was you. I'd give it up altogether."

It happened that Mrs. Brown had just been suggesting to Robert that he smoked too much, and Robert, thinking that William had overheard the conversation, turned on him indignantly.

"Well, I'm not going to, so you can shut up and mind your own business."

So ferocious did Robert sound that William decided to cease his appeal to his better self and took himself off as quickly as possible, shaking his head sadly over the effects of opium and cocaine upon the temper.

He made up his mind to find some means of handing Rupert Bergson over to justice without involving Robert, but it was several days before the opportunity presented itself.

It happened that the whole family, including the maids, was going to a display of local talent in the Village Hall, and that at the last moment Rupert Bergson, who had suddenly developed a cold in his head, said that he could not go with them.

"It's dod kide to go addywhere wid a code like dis," he said. "I'd rather stay at hobe."

"All right," agreed Robert, "and if you want anything to do you might clear out that old cupboard in my room—the one where my old cups and things are."

No sooner had the family taken its seats in the Village Hall than William, very quietly and unobtrusively, slipped from his chair and set off homeward again. In any case he was not interested in local talent. No one noticed that he had gone.

He opened the front door of his home and, creep-

151

ing up the stairs, peeped cautiously through the half-open door of Robert's bedroom.

There upon the floor knelt Rupert Bergson, conscientiously engaged in clearing out the cupboard. Around him on the floor stood various cups that had been won by Robert in his schooldays and, after being kept on the dining-room sideboard for several years, had been relegated to Robert's bedroom cupboard owing to complaints from the domestic staff about the time they took to clean.

William crept downstairs again and out into the road. His next step was to find the policeman but, as generally happens on such occasions, the policeman was not to be found. At last, however, William found him standing outside the Blue Lion lost in gloomy contemplation of his own boots.

"I say! Come quick!" said William. "There's a burglar in our house!"

The policeman turned startled eyes upon him.

"A what?" he said.

"A burglar," said William. "We'd all gone to the thing at the Village Hall, and I came home because—because I'd forgotten my handkerchief, and I found a burglar in Robert's bedroom."

"Where?" said the policeman. He spoke eagerly, and his whose aspect brightened. His life since joining the police a year ago had been one long and bitter disillusionment. He had not even been able to catch a motorist with his tail light out.

"Where?" he repeated. "Take me there quickly."

William took him to the house, led him up the stairs, and flung open the door of Robert's bedroom.

Rupert Bergson sat on the floor in front of the open cupboard surrounded by Robert's cups.

"That's him," said William.

"Now then, what are you doing with those cups?" said the policeman sternly to Rupert Bergson.

Rupert Bergson looked at him in surprise.

"I'b tidyig the cupboard," he explained.

Rupert sat in front of the cupboard, surrounded by Robert's cups. "That's him," said William.

"That's a nice tale!" said the policeman scornfully. "What are you doing in this house at all?"

"I'b stayig here," said Rupert Bergson. "I'b stayig in the house."

The policeman turned to William.

"He isn't," said William firmly.

"I'b stayig with his brother," said Rupert indignantly. "I'b his brother's friend. I'b been here for over a week."

William met his gaze unblinkingly.

"No, he isn't," he said. "I've never seen him before."

"You see it's no use making up tales like that," said the policeman sternly to Rupert Bergson. "You'd better come quietly."

William's plan was working out more successfully than he had dared to hope. He had thought that if he could get Rupert arrested for burglary with evidence of his drug trafficking guilt upon him (and he was sure to have evidences of his drug trafficking guilt upon him) he would be delivered over to justice without Robert's coming into it at all.

"And he's a drug trafficker, too," went on William excitedly. "You look in his pockets and I bet you find some."

Rupert Bergson's utter bewilderment gave him all the appearance of guilt. The policeman plunged his hand into his coat pocket and brought out the paper folded into the shape of a cocked hat that William had seen thrown upon the station platform.

"That's it," shouted William triumphantly. "Open it. You'll find cocaine in it."

"Id's an oudrage," said Rupert Bergson furiously.

The policeman had opened the paper and was slowly reading out the words that were written on it:

"Translate II. 260-360 and comment on the following constructions, giving parallel examples where possible."

At that moment there came the sound of footsteps and voices from the hall. The Browns were returning from the entertainment. Local talent, though well meaning, was limited, and William had taken a long time to find the policeman. They came upstairs and stood in an amazed group at Robert's door, gazing at William, the policeman, and the distraught Rupert Bergson. The policeman was still studying the note with a puzzled expression.

"What on earth's all this?" said Mr. Brown.

"Good Lord!" said Robert looking at the paper in the policeman's hand. "Why, it's the test paper."

"What test paper?" said Mrs. Brown weakly.

"Bergson's cousin was with some men at a reading party, and they'd got their tutor to set them a test paper to do at the end, and we thought we'd like to try our hand at it, too, as we've been doing the same book, so we asked Bergson's cousin to let us have it, and as his train went through the station here he said he'd chuck it out as he passed—less trouble than posting it. So he did, and we fagged through it that afternoon. But what on earth——?"

"An oudrage, I tell you," repeated Rupert Bergson fiercely.

The policeman was beginning to look as mystified as the rest of them.

"Well, this boy——" he began.

Then he turned round to look for William.

But William was nowhere to be seen.

William was in fact already little more than a dot on the distant horizon.

*Have you read
the other*

WILLIAM

*books published
by Armada?*

There is no other boy in fiction quite like William. Richmal Crompton's stories about him have been popular since the 1920's – and he's still a hero of readers today. There are scores more of his hilarious adventures in these Armada books. Have you got them all?

JUST—WILLIAM
WILLIAM—THE BOLD
WILLIAM'S HAPPY DAYS
WILLIAM'S CROWDED HOURS
WILLIAM—THE BAD
WILLIAM—THE DETECTIVE
SWEET WILLIAM
WILLIAM—THE GANGSTER
WILLIAM—THE OUTLAW
WILLIAM CARRIES ON
MORE WILLIAM
WILLIAM IN TROUBLE
WILLIAM—THE REBEL
WILLIAM AGAIN

From Alfred Hitchcock,

Master of Mystery and Suspense—

A thrilling series of detection and adventure. Meet The Three Investigators – Jupiter Jones, Peter Crenshaw and Bob Andrews. Their motto, "We Investigate Anything", leads the boys into some extraordinary situations – even Jupiter's formidable brain-power is sometimes stumped by the bizarre crimes and weird villains they encounter. But with the occasional piece of advice from The Master himself, The Three Investigators solve a whole lot of sensational mysteries.

Armada

The Hardy Boys Adventure Stories
by Franklin W. Dixon

The escapades of Frank and Joe Hardy, sons of a famous
detective, and their staunch friend, Chet Morton, lead
to breathtaking dangers and adventures. If you can't
resist a gripping plot, daring heroes, death-dealing
villains, hair's-breadth escapes and plenty of action, the
Hardy Boys are for you!

Armada

CAPTAIN ARMADA

has a whole shipload of exciting books for you

Armadas are chosen by children all over the world. They're designed to fit your pocket, and your pocket money too. They're colourful, gay, and there are hundreds of titles to choose from. Armada has something for everyone:

Mystery and adventure series to collect, with favourite characters and authors – like Alfred Hitchcock and The Three Investigators. The Hardy Boys. Young detective Nancy Drew. The intrepid Lone Piners. Biggles. The rascally William – and others.

Hair-raising spinechillers – ghost, monster and science fiction stories. Super craft books. Fascinating quiz and puzzle books. Lots of hilarious fun books. Many famous children's stories. Thrilling pony adventures. Popular school stories – and many more exciting titles which will all look wonderful on your bookshelf.

You can build up your own Armada collection – and new Armadas are published every month, so look out for the latest additions to the Captain's cargo.

If you'd like a complete, up-to-date list of Armada books, send a stamped, self-addressed envelope to:

Armada Books,
14 St James's Place,
London SW1A 1PF